'A cold coming we had of it,
Just the worst time of the year
For a journey, and such a long journey:
The ways deep and the weather sharp,
The very dead of winter.'

T. S. ELIOT

THE VERY DEAD OF WINTER

A family gathers for Christmas at a cottage in the depths of the country and in the dead of winter. Confined by the snow in the enchanted but threatening landscape of an ancient forest, they are drawn into a strange drama which unfolds around the enigmatic presence of the dying Konrad. Florence, his wife, views his impending death with annoyance and some grief. Their two children still bear the scars of this imperfect union, Anita scorning the world, Nicholas avoiding commitment. At the heart of the drama is the relationship between Florence and her unorthodox sister Sophia, who guards a startling secret yet remains benevolently aloof from the turmoil around her. Mary Hocking uncovers the foibles of human nature with remarkable insight, sympathy and a wit as sharp as winter holly.

THE VERY DEAD OF WINTER

Mary Hocking

CHIVERS LARGE PRINT
BATH

British Library Cataloguing in Publication Data available

This Large Print edition published by Chivers Press, Bath, 1994.

Published by arrangement with Chatto & Windus Ltd.

U.K. Hardcover ISBN 0 7451 2139 X
U.K. Softcover   ISBN 0 7451 2151 9

The epigraph on p. v is from 'Journey of the Magi' by T. S. Eliot, *Collected Poems 1909–1962*, and is quoted by permission of Faber & Faber Ltd.

Photoset, printed and bound in Great Britain by
Redwood Books, Trowbridge, Wiltshire

CHAPTER ONE

The beginning of the journey had been enchanting. Porcelain blue sky and the sparkling white canopy transformed dingy streets into fantasies of unimaginable purity and, passing out of the town, they came to broad fields where sunlight reflected a trellis of branches like veins across the snow. But as they drove, the small towns and villages, the farms, fields and hedgerows blurred, became intermittently discernible, and finally dissolved and there was only a moving whiteness against a grey background, as if a great speckled blind were being drawn endlessly down into a bottomless well.

'Who says there isn't a hell?' Anita said.

But Florence had kept a little store of excitement hidden away within her, and when at last the trees closed around them, she sang out, 'There was a house, once upon a time, in a wood. Oh, I feel a child again!'

'You've never stopped being one.' Her daughter was in no mood for singing.

'We used to come here every Christmas. It seemed quite magical.'

'If you've said that once you've said it ten times since we turned off the main road.' On either side branches heavy with snow reached over the path, poised like teasing

1

boys to unleash their load when least expected. 'I'm not convinced that was the main road.'

'There were the radio masts; you saw them yourself.'

'I can hardly see anything, the light is so bad. We should have set out earlier.'

Florence rubbed at the windscreen with the back of her glove. 'Aren't those car tracks? That's probably Nicholas.'

'He should have been here hours ago.' The windscreen wipers were having difficulty lifting their burden and each sweep left a thin powder encrusted on the glass. 'I hope it's not going to ice up before we get there. What a journey for poor Father. Why didn't you drive him down here yourself?'

'In this weather? If anything had happened what would I have done?'

'What do you think Nicholas would do?'

'If he can go up the Himalayas with a pack on his back, he can certainly carry his father through a snowy wood.'

'If it's as hazardous as that, why bring him here? It was you who came as a child, not he. This place means nothing to him.'

The path twisted, boring deeper into the forest. Something darted in front of the bonnet and Florence braked cautiously. 'What was that? It was too big for a fox.'

'A deer, I expect. Or would you fancy a bear? Keep going! Once the engine stalls we'll never get it going again.' The car lurched as it bumped over stones and boulders concealed by snow but still a hazard. When they came to a smoother patch, Florence said, 'Your father did come here once, before Nicholas was born. I thought he wouldn't remember, but when I was packing his things last night I came across a little sketch he had done of the cottage.'

'Who owned it then?'

'My family, of course.'

'There's no "of course" about it. The cottage didn't feature much in the stories of your childhood.'

'Your granny lived here until she had a stroke in 1961. Then it was sold—to pay for the nursing home.'

'And?'

Florence leant forward, peering ahead with pleated lips.

'If you're so reluctant to talk about this, why are we coming here?'

'Sophia bought it back again. That must have been when you were ten.'

'I remember. I was reading the Ashdown Forest books and I wanted to stay in a forest.'

'I wouldn't have let you stay with Sophia at that age.'

'So why do we have to come now, when I don't want to any more?'

3

Florence was looking from side to side and did not reply. Anita persisted, 'And what was so bad about Aunt Sophia—except that she gave up being a silversmith, which is hardly a crime—that I couldn't stay with her? I'd be happier if you looked ahead while you answer.'

'Sophia is very unpredictable. And it may not have been a crime to give up that job in London—the firm was very prestigious—but it was certainly perverse. I'd have had no idea what she might have got up to with you.'

'You mean she might have abused me?'

'Certainly not. People didn't do that kind of thing then.'

'In the seventies? How much do you bet me?'

'Well, our kind of people didn't do it. And, in any case, I always suspected she exchanged one craft for another.'

'Witchcraft?'

Florence steered the car towards what seemed no more than a thinning of the trees. The light gave way to a murky porridge which seemed all too appropriate to a witch's hearth. Florence said, 'I can see car tracks. I knew I was right.'

'The fact that there are other lunatics abroad doesn't prove anything.'

The snow was thinner here and a stubble of briars thrust through the whiteness. Anita

4

relaxed, grateful for this assurance of earth beneath. 'So Aunt Sophia's not a witch any more, is that it? She's reformed.'

'She is grown older and wiser.'

'How do you know? You haven't seen or spoken to her in over thirty years, not since my christening.'

Florence did not answer. Anita said, 'You just want her to have changed because it suits your purpose to come here. It's you who believes in magic. You wave your wand and things are just as you wish them to be.'

Florence began to hum 'In the bleak midwinter.'

'Why does it suit your purpose for us to come here now? Why, after all these years, do we have to come when Daddy is going to die and we'd all be better off in Chiswick?'

Florence rubbed the windscreen and bent forward, her breath misting the glass. 'I thought that Sophia should see him before...'

'You can't say it, can you? You can't even say that he's going to die. You're so afraid. That's why you've brought him here; so that you don't have to manage Christmas alone.'

'As I said, I thought Sophia should see him. After all, she is one of the family. And you're wrong. I *have* seen her since your christening. She was at Great Aunt Edith's funeral.' She braked as sharply as the snow permitted. 'Out you go, my treasure. There's

5

a branch across the track. It's a good job one of us looks ahead.'

'This is going to finish me. I've got my period as well as being nearly frozen to death.'

'A little exercise will do you no harm. Your generation gives up much too quickly.' As Anita fumbled with the seat belt, Florence gave an exclamation of impatience. She opened the car door and tumbled into a drift of snow at the edge of the track.

'There's no need to be in such a hurry. I'm coming.'

'You had best stay there now. Move into the driving seat.'

In the light of the headlamps Florence was revealed as a big, pear-shaped woman who moved majestically and spoke forcefully as if there were indeed bears to keep at bay. She bent down and dragged the branch out of the way; then capered about to show how pleased she was with her efforts. Anita called out, 'Don't imagine I'm going to carry you if you fall and break a limb.'

Florence came panting to the car door. 'Keep the engine running.' She was aware how much she irritated her daughter and deliberately repeated an overworked childhood joke. 'I'm going into the wood to be a good puppy.'

Anita sat with her brow resting on the steering wheel until her mother returned.

'You do realise this track is going downhill?' she said. 'Is that what it should be doing?'

'I think so.'

'You're not relying on your memory, I hope. Aunt Sophia did send a map.'

'We took the first turning on the left, as directed.'

'I'll take your word for it.'

The car crept forward, both women staring anxiously ahead into what was becoming a very gloomy scene.

'You must be prepared for your aunt to be rather odd,' Florence said. 'The clothes she affects...'

'What do you mean "affects"? Does she do something other than wear them?'

'You know quite well what I mean. In the country, I concede, a tweed skirt may not be so essential nowadays. Women do seem more comfortable in trousers—though why they wear jeans as tight as armour, I can't imagine.'

'Armour wasn't tight, just bulky.'

'But your aunt used to dress like a druid, or...'

'A witch.'

Florence cast a sidelong glance into the trees as though something might be hiding among them capable of understanding human speech. The windscreen wipers had stopped. Anita pressed the water jet button but nothing happened. 'I must have been mad to let you talk me into this.'

'There!' Florence cried excitedly. 'To the right—a clearing. And a lighted window, surely?'

Anita wound down the window the better to see. 'There seems to be fencing along here. I nearly ran into a post.' She stopped the car but did not immediately open the door.

Florence said impatiently, 'What are you waiting for?'

'I wish I hadn't come.' Anita got out. The sky had cleared and it was bitterly cold. In the half-light she could see the low stone house which had once been three foresters' dwellings, hunched beneath an overhang of snow. One weak light glimmered at a window. 'I bet it's freezing in there,' she said apprehensively. 'Does she have electricity? That looks like an oil lamp.'

Beneath the trees another, even lower, building was just visible, a thumbline smudge on the snow. 'Is that the hut where Nicholas is to sleep? It'll be a home from home for him, won't it?'

The door of the cottage opened and a figure stood on the threshold, a lamp in one hand.

'Like one of those spirits that greet the souls of the dead,' Anita said.

'Not with that lamp. Heaven is light perpetual.'

'Who said anything about Heaven?'

*   *   *

Anita sat on the edge of the bed. She couldn't remember being so cold in a house before; the houses she inhabited were all centrally heated. Her survey failed to trace a radiator. The only hope of heating appeared to lie in the small fireplace. Anita was accustomed to seeing dried flowers in grates. Her mother, whose bones were well covered, would make light of the cold; but how did Sophia, thin as a wire, manage to survive? The gaiety of the eyes, glinting like mica in the pointed face, suggested that survival presented no problem. Incredible that these two were sisters. Anita could hear them talking on the landing.

'I don't remember it like this when we came here as children,' Florence was saying.

'Our expectations were different.'

'I don't believe it's the same house.'

'We aren't the same people.'

'And it's so cold.'

'Our minds weren't preoccupied with heat and sanitation.'

'The sanitation is in working order, I trust.'

There was dim light from the oil lamp on the landing. If Anita turned her head she might glimpse them—Sophia in her element,

9

grey hair cascading on to the shoulders of the voluminous patchwork gown which seemed not an affectation but so appropriate to her it would be difficult to visualise her otherwise; Florence, not enhanced, a brighter light needed to reveal the compact bulk of her.

As they went down the stairs, Florence was saying, 'You must be a Commoner now, since you own the cottage. Do you exercise your right of pasturage, or whatever it is? I used to think it such a shame that Granny didn't have sheep and goats and several ponies. Not pigs. I wouldn't have ...' Her voice faded away.

Anita continued to sit hump-backed, fingers gripping the edge of the bed. She had been given a candle but had not lit it. It seemed to represent occupation, like a key to a hotel bedroom, and she did not want to be an occupant of this room let alone of this house. If it weren't for the snow, and the fact that they had come in her mother's car, she would pack up and leave. She stared down at her feet, mutinous and powerless as she had been most of her life. I am always finding myself pushed into a place where I don't want to be, she said to her feet.

It was getting colder. There was a respectable log fire burning in the hall and Sophia had said that tea would be ready soon; but once participate and one would become a player in this ridiculous charade.

10

Anita was reluctant to move in case this led to performance. She was afraid. It was ridiculous, of course, but she was unable to dispel the notion that at some stage on the journey from Chiswick she had crossed a line dividing the adult world from the world which exists only in the anarchic minds of children. The little hunched-down house, the unlikely sisters, the dying man in the room at the turn of the stairs, the ghostly white trees beyond the window, all conspired to present an image of a place where things would not proceed according to any set of rules with which she was familiar. Anita relished having rules to break.

Her mother would be of little comfort; she was only too eager to escape into another world during the time of Father's decline. As for Nicholas, he would make off into the snow on any pretext. Already he was out on some absurd errand, fetching a 'little man' who would restore normal lighting. It would take more than a forest gnome to do that; the weight of the snow had undoubtedly brought down a cable and they would be in semi-darkness all over Christmas.

Sophia, then—what could be expected of her in the way of reassurance? Anita considered Sophia, so much reported on, yet still unexpected. As she stood at the door to greet her guests, she had seemed to radiate energy of another order to that which

Florence expended. When Anita crossed the threshold, Sophia had looked at her as if they already knew each other, and mischief had bubbled to the surface as she smiled her welcome. Anita did not like being known, she had enough of that from her mother. There were matters she kept hidden, one of which was how afraid she was most of the time.

Dear God, if only the light would come on, obliterating all the shadowy corners!

'Tea is served,' Florence called from the foot of the stairs. She sounded exuberant. This was obviously the euphoric period of her reunion with Sophia.

Anita got up. The act of moving, rather than her brain, told her where she must go.

She had never known a fire in a bedroom and when she entered the room where her father lay she was inexplicably moved by the rosy light flickering on the wall. The tears, long held back, stung her eyes. The imminence of loss overwhelmed her. There was so much she had failed to share with her father, realms unimagined and therefore never explored which she would not enter now. How can you do this to us? she thought, looking at his sleeping face which was like a huge mask, pocked and discoloured by time. How can you go away, taking so much of you that we never knew?

She had always found him easier than her

mother precisely because he made no demands, attempted no forays into her private world. In her unrestful, agitated childhood he had been a great benign presence, comforting because always there, seeming to have just the resources needed to meet the events of her particular moment and nothing left to spare. She had thought: one day we will explore together, when I am older, when I am more confident, when I feel safer. He was the only person she would have trusted to lead her into a snowy wood on a December night and he was powerless to help her now.

She had told herself she must come into the room to see if he was all right, but she was not deceived: she had come to ensure that he was still there and in the hope that he might still answer her needs. It was herself with whom she was concerned, not the easing of his passage. 'Being self-critical is no good to anyone if you are not prepared to do anything about it,' Florence had pointed out on more than one occasion. How true, Anita thought, bending to kiss the hand that lay on the coverlet.

*   *   *

As she made toast, Sophia said to Florence, 'Anita is quite a beauty with that splendid mane of hair.'

'A tangle of red hair doesn't make a beauty; in fact, Anita's appearance would be greatly improved were she to accept that the Pre-Raphaelite look is definitely for the early twenties and put her hair up.' Florence's pale golden hair started the day with good intentions, swept into a neat knob on the top of her head from which it spent the remainder of the day detaching itself. 'Grooming is important when one gets older,' she said, impervious to her own condition. 'With that long straight nose Anita has quite the classical Greek look. All that is needed is some attention to her hair.'

'Not so fashionable to be classical Greek, though.'

'Oh, fashion! It's fashionable for older women to make the worst of themselves now, pathetically trying to do what youth does best. I fail to understand why liberated women—so called—are so anxious to look like teenage sex symbols. Long hair is a folly on an older woman.'

'Really?' Sophia stared into her cup, considering this statement gravely as though her own hair were not in question.

'Yes,' Florence said. 'Definitely a folly. But then Anita is immature. That's why she chose educational, rather than clinical, psychology.'

'You mean, she would have put her hair up had she opted for clinical psychology?'

Sophia asked demurely.

'She could hardly deal with adults looking like a cross between the Blessed Damozel and Alice in Wonderland.'

'But Anita is only just over thirty, surely. And perhaps this man Terence likes her hair the way it is.'

'Terence is another folly.' Florence wiped a dribble of butter from her chin. 'Why she insisted that he join us here, I can't imagine. He hates the country.'

'As they live together, I suppose...'

'She says he would have hated to spend Christmas on his own. But he wouldn't have spent it on his own, not him. Someone would have taken pity on him—some woman. He's very good at arranging to be pitied is Terence. I sometimes think that's how they came together in the first place—they both need someone to lean on. That's why he's coming here for Christmas—because she's afraid to be without him. In fact, if I hadn't been very firm and said I couldn't possibly do the journey on my own, she would have come on Christmas Eve with him.'

'He will have a difficult journey.' It was the first mention Sophia had made of travelling conditions.

'I had a difficult journey,' Florence said.

* * *

15

Tea had been served in the hall. Anita, coming down the stairs, hoped this did not mean there was no fire in the sitting-room.

'You haven't taken off your jacket,' Florence said, as if Anita might not have noticed.

'I'm frozen.'

'You should have come down sooner instead of mooning about up there in the dark.'

Florence and Sophia were seated one on either side of the hearth, Sophia like some bright fungus sprouting from the floor, Florence, plump legs outstretched, face scarlet, happy as Billy Bunter at a midnight feast.

'Come and join us. You can sit on the rug and make your own toast.' Florence took the teapot from the hearth and filled a cup for Anita. 'I've been telling Sophia that we must have a party.' She was eager to take charge. 'There must be people around here whose arrangements have been messed up by the snow who are wondering what on earth to do with themselves.'

'They probably don't want to venture out,' Anita said.

'Nonsense! It's only townsfolk who fuss about the weather.'

'There's Frances,' Sophia mused. 'She would probably be glad to come to a party, poor lamb.'

16

'There you are! And I expect there are several others besides this Frances who would be delighted to come.'

Sophia smiled a sidelong smile, eyes reviewing her sister. Mother isn't really in charge, Anita thought; she is simply being permitted to play, like a child allowed up late for Christmas. She turned the bread on the fork. 'There can't be that many people in this part of the forest, surely?'

'Enough for a party,' Florence said. 'There's a house not far from here, isn't there, Sophia? Down in the hollow by the stream.'

'Yes. Thomas Challoner lives there with his grandson and Frances.'

'Who or what is Frances?' Anita asked. 'And why a poor lamb?'

'Her sister married the Challoners' son. She produced one child, Andrew, and then took her leave, saying she was unsuited to motherhood and the boy would be better off without her. The young husband decided he wasn't better off and killed himself. The Challoners looked after the boy. Two years ago, Mrs. Challoner died.'

'What about the other grandparents?' Anita asked.

'They died years ago.'

'A lot of death in this family,' Florence commented disapprovingly.

'And Frances?' Anita's voice was sharp.

17

This story was not pleasing to mother or daughter.

'Frances came to see Thomas and Andrew through a bad patch and realised she had to stay.'

'How old is she?' Florence asked, not greatly impressed by such devotion.

'About twenty-two, I suppose.'

'She must be mad,' Anita said. 'That little lot won't be much fun at a party.'

Sophia looked at her, head a little to one side, as if she understood what occasioned this sudden sharpness and was inviting Anita to laugh about it—a 'you've been eating green apples again' sort of look.

'Now, who else can we muster?' Florence asked Sophia.

While they talked, Anita sat on the rug, buttering toast. The lamp did not give a strong light and it was some time before she noticed that a cat was sitting on the chest by the front door—a chocolate brown cat who sat upright, front paws neatly together, so still he might have been a carving had not the slanting green eyes blinked as she clicked her fingers.

'Tobias is Burmese,' Sophia said. 'He would like to be a cuddly, well-mannered cat, but he has personality problems.'

'What a nonsensical way to talk about a cat.' Florence hauled herself to her feet with some difficulty. 'Come and join us, Tobias.

18

You know you are longing to sit by the fire.'
She swept the cat into her arms.

By the time first aid had been rendered
and Florence had washed out her jumper,
Nicholas had arrived with the forest gnome.

★ ★ ★

Brother and sister were alone in the
sitting-room. Anita was piling logs on the
fire, watched uneasily by Nicholas, snow
glinting in his curly hair.

'Steady on!'

'I am determined we shall be warm even if
you have to cut down a tree.'

'Green wood won't burn,' Nicholas said
absently. He was a tamed Viking, the ferocity
smoothed out of the face; the nose become
sensitive, the nostrils slightly pinched; the
slash of the mouth softened by a need to
apologise. This gentling of the features had
produced a chronic hesitancy. The pale eyes
seemed to be constantly searching the
horizon for something which had been lost
over centuries.

'Don't fret,' Anita said, looking up at him
affectionately.

'How are things going?' He made a motion
of his head in the direction of the hall.

'Blood has already been drawn. There's
tea still stewing if you fancy it.'

'I think I've earned something stronger.'

He opened the door of a small cupboard built underneath the stairs. Anita saw a vacuum cleaner, brooms and several bottles on the floor.

'How did you know where to look?'

'Father had a whisky when we got here.'

'Was that good for him?'

'Sophia said anything he wanted was good for him.' He hesitated, as though wondering whether to add to this statement, then turned away and poured whisky for himself. 'What about you?'

'I haven't the excuse that I've been fetching and carrying.'

'I don't think Sophia would consider an excuse necessary.' He poured a good measure, and handed the glass to Anita.

'That sounds as if you had some understanding of Sophia, which is more than I have.'

'She struck me as the sort of person who doesn't require understandings.'

Anita shrugged and turned away. 'How are conditions outside?'

'Tricky, but one can still get about. The snow has stopped.' He went to the window, crouching to look out. 'In fact, it's quite magical, here in the wood—like a fairy story.'

'I hate fairy stories.'

'Do you?' He looked at her with interest, as if this were something he should have known. It was charming, this gift he had of making other people's little oddities seem a matter of friendly concern. 'I was hoping we might go for a walk later on.'

'I may. Anything to get out of here for a little while.'

'That's what I thought.'

Anita sipped whisky. 'And there may be an opportunity. Mother has decided we are to have a party, and as telephone wires are probably down, it could be a question of delivering invitations by hand. A chance for us to show Christmas goodwill, don't you think?'

In the event, the telephone was found to be working and Sophia managed to contact several people, all of whom professed themselves pleased (or curious, Anita wondered) at the prospect of meeting Florence and family. The Challoners' phone gave the unobtainable signal. 'You're not the only witch,' Anita thought, as Sophia put down the receiver after the third attempt. 'I willed that.'

Florence, who was making a list of delicacies, said 'I hope you don't cook by electricity?'

The little gnome had long since been taken home, recompensed though defeated.

'Neither gas nor electricity.'

'A cauldron?' Anita suggested.

'A perfectly respectable Aga.'

21

*　　*　　*

When Nicholas and Anita set out for the Challoners' house Sophia stood at the sitting-room window, watching them make their slow way across the garden. Tobias, curled around her shoulders, purred nasally. Florence was upstairs with her husband. She had delayed seeing him earlier because 'I mustn't disturb Konrad when he's resting—it is so good for him to rest.'

There was no light in the room, save the last glow from the logs in the hearth. The window was beginning to frost over and Sophia opened it, the better to see out. It was a cold, glittering night, the trees silvery cones of snow, the sky brilliant. 'Such a multitude of stars tonight,' she said. 'Will they find their way?' Tobias pushed his head against her cheek. 'It is a long time since we have had this many people here, but you must not express your displeasure so markedly. We must be kind to these poor children.'

Nicholas and Anita had only just reached the palings which were the boundary of the garden. The snow was deep but they were both tall and could have made better progress had they so wished. Now, they turned to look back at the cottage. 'They are troubled,' Sophia said, scratching Tobias's head.

'I don't want to go back there,' Anita said.
'It will be better in the morning.'

'No, it'll be much worse. Mother will have us all preparing for this stupid party.'

'But that's no different from any other Christmas,' he said gently.

'This will be macabre instead of irritating.'

He put his hand under her elbow, urging her forward. 'You're enjoying this,' she said. 'Now that you're out of doors you feel safe. You don't even have to sleep in that cottage.'

'As a matter of fact, I do. Sophia is sleeping in the hut. She was very insistent.'

'That's taking hospitality a bit far.'

'I got the impression it wasn't a question of hospitality.'

'What then?'

'I don't think she wanted me in the hut.'

Anita stumbled and caught her breath. 'I like this less and less.'

'People have their funny ways.' He veered away from controversy. 'I sleep in the sitting-room. No problem.'

'I had hoped you'd be in the hut and I could come and talk to you—get away from the cottage.'

'You'll have Terence.'

'Terence won't put his nose out of doors once he gets here. Even before the snow started he felt he was making a considerable

23

sacrifice coming here. Goodness knows what sort of mood he'll be in by the time he arrives tomorrow.'

'Tell me about the people we're going to meet.'

Anita stopped. 'I had forgotten.' She looked at the shrouded trees. 'We're never going to find our way there, and even if we do we shan't get back.'

'Don't be silly. This isn't trackless moorland. The trees mark paths.'

'But they're all alike now.'

'Of course they're not.' He spoke as to a child. 'The pointy ones are firs and they still have their leaves; look how the snow bunches between the leaves. The skeletal ones are birch and oak and you can see their bark in spite of the snow.'

'All right, all right. I'll allow that you can find the way back. But how do we find the way forward when neither of us has ever been to the Challoners' house?'

'We're going downhill and we'll come to a stream. The house will be beside the stream. Nothing simpler.'

She stood still, a hand to her chest. 'I haven't any breath.'

'Wrap your scarf across your nose.'

'I'll have even less breath then.'

'No. It'll warm you.'

'I'm going to die, like Daddy.'

He put his arms round her. 'Oh, Annie,
24

don't!'

Something moved in the snow; yellow eyes glanced and vanished.

'What was that?' Anita gasped.

'A fox. Look where his brush has swept the snow.'

Anita, still holding close to her brother, said, 'Didn't you hate taking him in the car? All that time alone, with him so ill?'

Nicholas, looking over her shoulder into the snowy depths of the wood, replied, 'I thought I would, but he was quite content—as if he was looking forward to coming here. We hardly spoke, there seemed no need. It was very peaceful.'

He thrust Anita away from him abruptly. 'Come along. It can't be far now.' He strode ahead without looking to see if she followed. 'We're lucky to have a night like this. No ugly glow from the town, only the light of the stars.'

'That's all very well for a time; but when you come back after one of your expeditions, would you really want to be without all modern comforts?'

'It depends what one finds comforting.'

She pursued him, treading in his footprints. 'And what would be the point of your away trips if things were just the same at home? Where would you run to Nicholas?' The path was going downhill steeply now and Anita lost her footing. After that she was

25

too concerned with her progress to badger her brother.

'There!' Nicholas pointed to a house in the hollow, clearly visible in the brightness of snow and stars. It was more substantial than their aunt's cottage, built sideways on to the stream, now still and glazed. The curtains had been drawn against the night and the house presented a blank face to the wood. 'Probably gone to bed early,' Nicholas said, uneasy at the prospect of causing inconvenience.

'I'm sure this Frances person will be making mince pies, or doing the ironing or attending to some other worthy task.'

'Who are these people?' He stood looking doubtfully down at the house, as though he hoped it might disappear beneath his scrutiny.

'Mr. Challoner, his grandson Andrew, and Andrew's mother's sister, who is by way of being a saint. Come on, let's get this over with.' She began to slither down the slope. Nicholas followed, more surefooted.

'But what if they've gone to bed?'

'Then we get them up. I haven't come all this way just to turn back now.'

'We could put a note through the letterbox.'

'So we could, but we're not going to.'

As they approached, a dog began to bark, the noise coming from a very deep chest.

'Let's hope he's under better control than Tobias.'

'This is awful,' Nicholas protested. 'We can't stand here and say we've come with this silly invitation.'

Anita knocked firmly on the door. The barking of the dog crescendoed. 'Yes we can. And it isn't going to sound awful; it's going to sound lovely and friendly and Christmassy, because you're going to do it with your unfailing charm.'

Footsteps crossed the hall. Nicholas gave a little whinny of agitation which was answered by furious snuffling from the far side of the door. 'Who is it?' a low voice asked.

'Sorry about this,' Nicholas said cheerfully. 'It's the people from the cottage up above—Sophia's nephew and niece.'

'Friends, Jasper, friends.'

The door opened and Nicholas found himself closely inspected by a huge mastiff, paws on his chest. 'You're a handsome fellow,' he said, looking into the bloodshot eyes.

'He won't hurt, but he likes to inspect rather than take my word. Come in.'

'Is that allowed?' Nicholas asked, looking over the dog's shoulder. 'And what about my sister?'

'She'll be all right now he's accepted you.'

The speaker remained masked by the

27

shadow of the door and Anita, imagining herself speaking to a child, said, in her professional voice designed to clarify and to reassure, 'I'm Anita Müller and this is my brother, Nicholas, and you must be...'

The shadow speaker said, 'I'm Frances,' and stepped into the light.

*　　　*　　　*

At first, Florence had read aloud to Konrad because this was something she was good at. She had crouched by the hearth, imagining she remembered doing that in this very room as a child, reading to Sophia by firelight. But she soon became very hot and her eyes smarted and the crouching position did not suit her ample body. She was annoyed by the fact that she had to roll herself to one side before she was able to get up. This was one of the many ways in which Konrad's illness had served to remind her of her own age. 'You are as young as you feel,' she told herself, standing by his bed, panting.

'That was very good.' His voice was laboured as a rusty hinge.

'I had to stop because there isn't a lamp in here. The electricity has gone off and we have to be sparing with the oil.'

'I like firelight in a bedroom.'

She wondered where his mind was. There had never been firelight in a bedroom in

28

their house in Chiswick. The adult Florence had soon equated fires with drudgery, and electric heaters had been installed in all the open hearths in the house. Now, usually brisk in dismissing any question of fires, she found herself obscurely disturbed by Konrad's rambling remark.

'I'm sure you didn't have a fire in your bedroom in Houndsditch. Is it Germany you're remembering?'

She could not account for the strong need she felt to track down the source of this memory. But the question, far from leading to clarification, seemed to remove a barrier to other questions which came flooding in. He had spoken so little of his past that she could not be sure it was Germany—could it have been Austria?—that he came from. Was she right about Houndsditch? And to what part of his early life did this firelit bedroom belong? For some reason, the image opened up a world as strange to her as a fairground or a circus.

'Where was it, this firelit bedroom?' she insisted. 'Was it a wood fire, coal, peat . . . ?'

But he only opened his eyes and gazed at the fire.

Florence's heart was beating fast and her hands were clammy. She went out of the room and called from the landing to her sister.

'You must come up and sit with us. It's

29

important we share this.' As Sophia came up the stairs, she said sharply, 'You're not bringing that animal with you?'

'He won't want either of us once he sees a bed.'

As it seemed that Tobias was the price which must be paid for Sophia's presence, Florence contented herself with grumbling, 'No one so far has expressed regret.'

'Tobias lives for the present. He knows nothing of regret.'

'He is a dumb animal, but his mistress can speak.'

'I have learnt to share Tobias's philosophy. And I did warn you. Tobias does not have retractile claws—it makes things difficult for him.'

Once in the bedroom Tobias disappeared under the eiderdown. A smile twitched the corners of Konrad's mouth. 'My little hot-water bottle is come.'

'He talks as though he is used to a cat on the bed.' Florence turned a face crumpled in bewilderment to her sister. 'How all this strangeness has come about, I don't know.'

Unintentionally, she had spoken of this strangeness as though it had been there before Konrad's illness, a process; she had given it recognition. Sophia, watching her sister's puzzled face, recalled hearing their mother say, 'There is so much that Florence fails to understand. I sometimes wonder whether she is deaf or stupid.'

'In any situation, Florence's desires are paramount,' their father had replied in that dry voice which sometimes betrayed a dislike of his children. 'The sun orbits Florence's globe. It makes any kind of objectivity impossible.'

'Why are you smiling?' Florence asked sharply.

'Was I smiling?'

'A horrid, sly smile. I should like to know what you find funny at this moment.'

'I was thinking of our misspent youth.'

'I fail to see the relevance of that to the present situation.'

But Florence was aware that in her youth she had been prone to misconceptions, of which Konrad Müller was the prime example. She had married Konrad in 1953. He had come to England as a refugee in the 1930s and looked foreign, formed from a different mould than Englishmen of her acquaintance who tended to be long in body and head, whereas Konrad's body was substantial without being fat and the head was big and round, the face broad with bluntly sculpted features. She was impressed by the sheer mass of him. A man like this, she had told herself, will go far. He was genial and would undoubtedly make a good travelling companion.

'There was talk of the diplomatic service at

one time, you know,' she said to Sophia.

'From him?'

'I don't recall if he actually mentioned it, or whether it was just mooted. I can't have made it up. I wanted it very much—tours of duty in European cities, Moscow in the snow, Paris in the spring, Corpus Christi processions in Seville; but I still wouldn't have made it up.' She frowned, wondering how she could have so totally misjudged the situation, and then turned from analysis as was her wont. 'You're quite right. There is nothing to be gained from regret. I see now that that has been my philosophy as well as Tobias's. Konrad went on working at the World Service and we lived an entirely uneventful life in Chiswick.'

'And he was satisfied?' The question was slipped in much as the child Sophia might have put out a foot to trip her older sister.

Florence was surprised that it was Konrad's satisfaction which should be the subject of attention. 'Satisfied? Oh, who knows about satisfaction? To be satisfied implies needs and hungers, desires, dreams even. I have no idea if Konrad had any of these things, so I can't say whether he was satisfied or not. He did not appear discontented.' She looked at him, lying now with his eyes closed. 'It happens a lot in marriage, Sophia, that the partners reach a certain point and realise they don't want to go any further. I have never known much about Konrad.'

There had been a time, at the beginning, when she had thought it would be different. He had seemed so unusual, without being quite other—an acquired taste, perhaps, but once acquired part of one's normal diet, like aubergine and Angostura bitters. But he had remained a stranger. Not that he deliberately withheld himself; it was more a matter of not conforming to her expectations. Her expectations were absolute. There had remained throughout her married life a picture of a husband who was not Konrad. 'I am not bitter,' she said. 'Bitterness never agreed with me, it lies on the stomach like bad wine.'

'And Konrad?' Sophia asked.

Florence shrugged. The Konrad who should have been was encapsulated in a space within her, a kind of Shangri-La of the spirit; what had happened to the real Konrad she did not know. 'I didn't reproach him,' she said.

She saw herself as a practical woman. 'Unhappiness suits me even less than bitterness.' She had set about the business of happiness much as she would have assembled the ingredients for a cake, ensuring that the nutritional content was well seasoned with spice. She had a taste for company, particularly male. She smiled, remembering the societies she had joined and the pleasures unrelated to their *raison d'être* which they had afforded her. Konrad had stayed at home.

'Konrad was never a joiner,' she said to Sophia. 'He spent a lot of his spare time painting on his own. He often went away on painting weekends.'

'Do you like his paintings?'

'I don't think they're good. He couldn't have exhibited them. They're quite unlike anything displayed at our local Arts Club.'

Konrad lay concentrating on his breathing, which required an effort he was less and less inclined to make. He heard the two sisters talking but could not make much sense of what was said. He had always had difficulty piecing things together. Now, lying here in this firelit room, the past came before him vividly, but disjointed.

He had been sent to England in 1937 when he was six years old. He never saw his parents again. He lived in Houndsditch with an aunt and uncle who had not wanted him but had not had the courage to refuse him. The experience had permanently disorientated him and he had great difficulty making a mental map of his environment— one street did not lead to another but existed in isolation. He was always getting lost. When the war came and the bombers broke up the patterns of streets he was cheered by

34

this experience of a shared chaos.

Florence was talking about her expectations. He remembered overhearing someone say that his had been a tragic childhood, but as no one had explained tragedy to him he had managed well enough. The people who looked after him, his aunt and uncle and teachers, did the best they could and he expected no more. In contrast to Florence, he was expectation free.

He had done various jobs when he left school, including set construction and painting at a small local theatre where he struck up an acquaintance with a man who was eventually responsible for his entering the World Service. The BBC was considered a rather glamorous place by his parish priest. At a Christmas party he had introduced Konrad to a young woman. 'This fellow has a great gift for languages. Sure an' it'll be the diplomatic service for him. Can you not see, with a great head like that, no doors will be closed to the man.'

Florence said, 'For years after I married him I expected that, having perfected his linguistic skills at the BBC, he would pass on to the diplomatic service.'

It was only when asked by a friend at the Arts Club what Konrad had read at university that she finally accepted the reality of Konrad's prospects. 'St. Vincent de Paul School, Mason Street, was his university,'

35

she had said and packed the diplomatic service off to Shangri-La.

'Do you remember St. Vincent de Paul, Mason Street?' she said, bending over Konrad.

He had done well at school. The perplexities of mathematical problems which were capable of solution appealed to him. He had a natural gift for languages. In his last year at school, when it was considered that some attempt should be made to 'stuff a little culture into the beggars', he painted. 'It would not be true to say that he learnt to paint,' his art master had written, 'rather that he suffered instruction.' Konrad gave a little rattle of laughter.

'You see,' Florence said triumphantly. 'He remembers St. Vincent de Paul.'

'His mind hasn't gone,' Sophia said. 'He's just very tired.'

'He was rambling before you came up.'

'What did he say?'

Florence could not now remember what had been said; only her unease remained in her mind. 'I'm tired,' she said, realising what a trying day it had been and how little concern had been expressed for her. 'I've had a bad journey.'

Sophia got up. 'You must go to bed. I'll wait up for Nicholas and Anita.'

'Why did they want to go out on a night like this?' Florence fretted as they went down to the kitchen.

'I expect Nicholas has been out on many a worse night.'

'Anita hasn't. She's very reluctant to exert herself at the best of times.'

Sophia poured milk into a saucepan and Florence wished she could have examined the saucepan before it made contact with the milk.

'Is this the worst of times, Florence?' Sophia asked gently.

'Only an unmarried woman could possibly ask such a question at such a time. My husband is going to die—letting go of life would be a better way of putting it. There is a treatment, you know. It would give him a little longer—I believe some people even have a couple of extra years. But he didn't want it. I am surrounded by people who let go. Nicholas is brilliant. He got a first in geology. He doesn't have to go off climbing mountains and drinking yak milk and sleeping in deserts. And Anita is wasting her time with Terence, who is also a time-waster.'

Sophia handed her sister a mug of hot milk.

'Is this mug clean? It's very stained.'

'Just old.'

'And what becomes of me? They none of them think of that.' Florence sipped the milk. 'I haven't heard you express sympathy so far.'

'I am sorry for you, Florence.'

*   *   *

There was a storm lamp on the table in the Challoners' kitchen which threw a stronger light than Sophia's oil lamps. Even so, Frances bent to make some adjustments—perhaps to cloak nervousness. Anita thought: she can't live up to that striking appearance, so she is playing for time, while Nicholas is looking at her as if he had uncovered a rare mural. Sophia might have given us some inkling of what to expect! Dark hair brushed back from a high forehead disdained curl or tendril which might have softened austerity; beneath dark eyebrows wide grey eyes gave to the face the look of a person awaiting, if not actually experiencing, a mystical event; the mouth was full and firm. A face any film director would be happy to cast as a nun and few Reverend Mothers would want as a novice.

'Would you like cocoa ... or a drink, perhaps?' Frances stepped back from the lamp but seemed uncertain where drinks might be located. Anita reflected how much she disliked women who didn't know how to serve drinks.

'Cocoa will do nicely,' Nicholas said.

Anita looked at him pityingly. What did he

think he was going to get out of this—the thrill of entering a forbidden temple? As Frances heated milk on the stove, Anita studied her, making mental jottings—unusually composed for her age: although she is nervous she doesn't allow herself to be hustled; emotionally reserved, but she can still look at Nicholas as if she is making a votive offering of this bloody cocoa; sexually unfulfilled, neither child nor woman. I wouldn't want to deal with her and Nicholas certainly shouldn't be allowed to.

Frances put a mug down in front of Anita without acknowledging her presence. The faintest of half-moons beneath her eyes suggested that in later years she would become interestingly haggard; and haggard, certainly, were the clear eyes which focused intently on whatever it was that claimed their attention—on this occasion, Nicholas.

'You must wonder why we are here,' Nicholas said, accepting the cup from Frances who did, indeed, look wondering. He delivered the invitation and Frances said she was sure they would be glad to accept.

'Thomas is out at a Commoners' meeting, but I'm sure he hasn't anything planned for tomorrow. Sophia did mention that her sister would probably want to have a party.'

Anita wondered what else Sophia had mentioned and Frances answered as surely as if the thought had been spoken, 'You're the child psychologist.' She did not say it as if it were a joke, but her tone did not suggest a profession to be taken seriously.

'And you're the explorer.' Her eyes examined the reality of Nicholas. 'I've read your books and heard you on radio and I saw you once on television.'

'Only the once. I don't go alone into the unknown with a camera crew trailing behind.' His smile was so disarmingly self-deprecating and the creases around the eyes suggested such a wealth of good humour that it was difficult to understand why people were so often shy in his presence. Frances, Anita noticed, was now unsure how to proceed.

'I find it difficult enough just getting shopping done in this snow,' she ventured. 'I can't imagine self-catering in the Arctic.'

'Neither can Nicholas,' Anita interposed. 'The Arctic is one of the wastes he hasn't explored.'

'I couldn't cope with Christmas preparations,' Nicholas assured Frances. 'The assembling of all the goods would be beyond me. But I'm quite a capable porter, if you need any help tomorrow.'

'But your mother...'

This was acceptance, Anita realised, and intervened, 'Most certainly Mother...'

'A combined trip, then,' Nicholas said, and before Anita could speak Frances

40

replied, 'That would be wonderful.'

Jasper, despair of humankind etched in fold and furrow, had been slumped against the stove, drooling on to his paws. Suddenly, he sat erect, the sense of expectation so strong that Anita's skin prickled.

The kitchen door swung open and for a nightmare moment it seemed that something out of a circus stood there, an elderly man in miniature, the slight body enfolded in a long, grey dressing gown. The hair was so fair it might have been silver; the eyes were blinkered by enormous glasses which required a wrinkling of the nose and a lopsided hitch of the upper lip to keep them in place and gave to the face an appearance of pernickety studiousness.

'Come in, Andrew,' Frances said. 'Friends have come to see us.' It struck Anita that there were echoes here of her earlier reassurance of Jasper.

The boy, whom Anita judged to be between six and seven, came forward a few paces and then stopped. The dog lumbered across to sit beside him, shoulder to shoulder, an ominous warning to potential evildoers.

'We're lost in the wood, like Hansel and Gretel,' Anita said to her brother, who seemed to her typecast for the foolish Hansel. 'What will befall us next?'

'It's the other house that's the gingerbread

41

house,' the boy said.

'The other house?'

'He thinks the cottage where you're staying is the gingerbread house,' Frances explained. 'But you don't think Miss Kimberley is a witch, do you?'

The boy seemed reluctant to have words put into his mouth. The dog gazed at him with mournful eyes, sharing a conspiracy of silence.

'The bad people in the fairy stories are so unconvincing.' Anita was not quite sure at whom she was aiming these remarks. 'They always give themselves away—too long a nose, too bright an eye. No intelligent child could possibly be taken in by them.'

'I read a story where the witch did eat Hansel and Gretel,' the boy said.

'That's not the usual version for children. How did you come by it?'

'A boy at school. His sister gave it to him. He can't sleep at night now in case the witch comes and eats him.' This explanation of the plight of his schoolmate did not appear to disturb Andrew.

'Do you sleep in those glasses?' Anita asked.

He gave her a sharp glance and looked away. Clear glass, she thought.

'We've been asked to a party at the gingerbread house,' Frances said. 'Won't that be fun?'

'Is Jasper coming?'

'No, Jasper is going to guard this house while we're away. The gingerbread house belongs to Tobias.'

The boy's face brightened at the mention of Tobias. This, Anita thought, is a child who has an affinity with threatening animals. Her reaction to him was a reminder that her understanding of children was not matched by a corresponding sympathy. She had studied child psychology because she had thought it might help her to resolve her own problems, but knowledge had not equated with healing.

The boy said to Frances, 'Is that lady going to be there?'

'A lot of people will be there. I think perhaps you should go back to bed, Andrew. Do you want to take hot milk up with you?'

His mouth twisted in knowing contempt. Anita's fingers itched to strike him, so much did he resemble her childhood self confronting authority with the only weapon it knew. Frances's response was to take him by the shoulders and march him out of the room. Jasper followed, presumably to ensure fair play. As they went up the stairs, Andrew said in a high, clear voice, 'I don't like that lady.' In a few minutes Jasper returned and flung himself down by the stove, his brow more deeply furrowed than ever.

'Hasn't had a Baskerville to eat in months,

poor old chap,' Anita said.

Nicholas looked at her, eyes squinting slightly as though the light from the lamp hurt. The whole face seemed to anticipate hurt. 'Perhaps we'd better go.'

'The fact that I haven't made a very good impression on a disturbed child doesn't trouble me.'

He finished his cocoa and went to the sink to wash the mug.

'You, on the other hand, seem to have made quite an impact.' Anita got up and put her hand on his shoulder. The dog growled. 'Oops! He's only my brother—nothing going on that could possibly offend you.'

Frances returned, looking flushed. 'I'm sorry to leave you. Andrew gets a bit difficult at Christmas—it's unsettling for him, I suppose—all the emphasis on family life and—'

'Would you like us to wait until Mr. Challoner gets back?' Nicholas asked.

'Oh no, I've got Jasper ... not that he, of course ... I mean, it's kind of you, but it's late and they'll be expecting you back at the cottage and ...' She ran on in confusion, Nicholas interjecting an occasional 'Oh no ...' 'Not at all...'

Anita, recognising a situation from which her brother would not extricate himself easily, said briskly, 'Well, then, we'll look forward to seeing you all tomorrow, about

44

noon.'

'You're sure you'll find the way?' Frances asked.

'There and back,' Nicholas assured her. 'I'll call tomorrow at nine o'clock to help with the shopping.'

'Well, if you're sure. That will leave Thomas free to go for a walk with Andrew, who does like to spend some time with him.' She opened the front door and began to rephrase her thanks, but Nicholas, scenting freedom, walked into the night.

'Thank you for the cocoa,' Anita said, moved to fellow feeling by the look of baffled resentment on Frances's face.

'Not a saint after all,' she said to Nicholas as they made their way into the wood. 'Just a Rapunzel in need of rescue. So what about it? You are a mountaineer and she has the rope.'

'Don't be silly, Annie.'

'Are you afraid those tresses might bind you?' She continued in mock dramatic vein while they climbed slowly upwards; then, needing to recover breath, turned to look to where the house lay beneath them. 'Even now, she's probably sitting by her bedroom window, brushing her hair and casting spells.'

Nicholas, who had been glancing from side to side as he walked as though searching for something, turned, and swinging her into

45

his arms, lofted her into the fork of a broken tree. 'I read a story once of someone being dropped into the trunk of a hollow tree from which they could never escape.'

Anita peered down at him, a latter-day Titania with twigs and dead leaves in her hair. 'How very unpleasant. Is that what you wish on me?'

'Who knows?'

His upraised face, pewter in moonlight, was indifferent and unfamiliar. It occurred to her there might be sacrifices he was prepared to make in order to protect himself.

'You wouldn't have the courage, Nicholas.'

'Don't put me to the test.'

How oddly courage and cowardice can be blended in one person, she thought, and said, 'Why are you so afraid? She's a little scrawny thing and I don't suppose her spells are very strong.'

He turned and walked away. One minute he was there, the next the white trees blotted out his figure. Anita leant forward, looking for the easiest way down. Suddenly, she began to scream, 'Pax, Nicholas, pax, pax ...' When he came back she was rocking from side to side on her perch, screaming. He hauled her down and she clung to him.

'There was blood on the snow, Nicholas. When was it? Do you remember?'

'No more nonsense.' He urged her

forward.

'It happened. Don't you remember? I looked down and there was blood on the snow.'

'Look up instead of down.' He was taking long strides, dragging her with him although she could barely keep her balance. 'You won't have many chances to see such a sky.'

'I hate this place. Give me a street lamp any time.'

He went on as if she had not spoken, 'The desert is best, of course...'

'If the desert is best, how come they don't know their good fortune, all these Arabs rolling up their tents and exchanging oil for sand?'

He pointed. 'See that great mound of snow on that boulder? Just beyond it you'll see the cottage.'

Sophia was waiting for them. She asked no questions about why they had been away so long, but gave each of them a hot toddy and a candle. As she went up the stairs, Anita wondered whether it was her imagination that the house smelt of gingerbread.

★   ★   ★

Sophia had been out to light the Calor gas stove in the shed so that the room would be warm when she went to bed. The flickering gas cast blue shadows, but when she came

47

out and shut the door no light penetrated the shutters over the windows. The shed looked as if there were no entry to it, a closed, secret place; yet it was well timbered and capacious and in summer must have opened out welcomingly on to the garden.

Sophia stood for a moment looking around, wondering if the old fox had come yet for the food she always put out for him. He was nearing his end and she would miss him when he no longer dragged his weary way to her door. She could see the footprints made by Nicholas and Anita, and a series of little arrows made by a bird. The snow, crisp now, clotted the trees; the flowerpots foamed and the lawn was a great ice floe surrounding the cottage. An owl perched motionless on the post of the garden gate.

She went round to the back of the cottage and into the scullery. Snow, melted from the boots that had been abandoned there, was now turning to ice. She wiped her own boots clean and fetched a kettle which had been warming on the Aga. 'We don't want any broken hips this Christmas,' she said to Tobias, who had come to complain because he was shut away from the bedroom. He slapped at her with an angry brown paw and she flicked the scrubbing brush at him. He walked away, lashing his tail and hissing at any obstacles in his path.

Once satisfied that she had taken

reasonable precautions, Sophia went into the dining-room to set the table for breakfast. 'You note we are eating in style tomorrow,' she said to Tobias, who was sulking on the stairs. 'So we must behave as if we knew how it was done. We have let things go a bit, you and I.'

When she had finished, she sat for a while in the kitchen, enjoying the hunched-down feel of a household under snow. 'This is a good time,' she said, stroking Tobias. 'A time when people are grateful for comforts they usually take for granted.' He bit her hand.

She thought about the morning, not as Florence might, making mental checks on provisions, but about the people who would come. Terence, in particular. Florence had made it sound as if he were no more than an escape route—from what, or whom, did Florence think her daughter was escaping? It would be interesting to meet the man on whom the beautiful Anita had bestowed herself. Then there was Andrew. She was glad that he would be here—there should always be children on Christmas Eve and in snow; children are so much better at celebrating than adults. She hoped Nicholas would take the boy out, carrying him on his shoulders through the wood, the erl-king and his child. The thought made her laugh. Her own pointed face, with the wide-spaced eyes which seemed always to glance askew and the smile like a slice of melon, had an elfin quality, but this was tempered by the broad, flattened nose which had a peasant robustness that earthed the humour.

The clock in the hall struck midnight. 'If you are very good I will take you up to Konrad,' she said to Tobias. She went into the hall and paused for a moment outside the sitting-room. There was no sound. Nicholas, however restless his spirit, was a quiet sleeper. Sophia climbed to the landing, placing her feet carefully, knowing every creaking tread; there the house divided, three bedrooms to the left at the front of the house and to the right, two steps down to one bedroom, the bathroom and a store cupboard. Konrad had been given the isolated bedroom because it was near the bathroom. She found him sitting by the fire. The night seemed to be his best time; a fact which Florence could not accept because it was contrary to medical experience. She considered this preference for the night to be yet another instance of Konrad's perversity. Sophia made no remonstrance, but seated herself on the hearth rug, knees drawn up. Tobias burrowed beneath the eiderdown.

'It must have been a hard journey,' she said.

'All our journeys are hard; mine has been no worse.' He frowned. 'That sounds ungrateful. There has been much for which to be grateful.'

Sophia took the poker to one of the logs, turning it to break the wood until the log fell apart and flames spurted up.

'Will it make things hard for you that it should happen here?' he asked.

'Where else? And it's time Florence came. We got on so well as children I used to think she was part of me. I remember Aunt Winifred saying, "It must be marvellous to have that lovely companionship available for life." I suppose at that age our differences didn't show—or didn't matter.' She gazed into the fire, chin on knees. 'It's only when we get older that it matters that other people are different.'

'It matters a great deal to Florence. She has so many certainties.'

'Certainty may not be good for us, do you think—not food? I wonder whether we'd grow at all if we lived in certainty.'

'I couldn't say. It's something I've never had. And I'm not likely to have it now, am I?'

'Oh, I'm not sure of that. You may be nearer to it than any of us.'

'But I don't know what I want to be certain about. Whereas Florence will go to her Maker with a list ready prepared.'

Sophia looked at him, studying the face in the firelight, which had the appearance of

51

being eaten into by the flames. 'You will go with other things, more important,' she said softly.

They sat in silence, both gazing into the fire, then Konrad said, 'She doesn't know, does she, Sophia?'

'I don't think so.'

'Will she have to?'

'She may.' She put her hand on his knee. '"And it came to pass ..." I always find that a very potent phrase, don't you? "And it came to pass that when Konrad was dying, Florence chose to spend that Christmas with her sister, Sophia."'

CHAPTER TWO

A bitter wind swirled up the high street, scything through the group of people huddled outside the closed door of Barclays Bank. A fair-haired man with the dimpled, pampered face of a baroque putto banged on the door.

'We've already done that,' a woman said, aggrieved by this presumption.

The door opened and the head of a young man appeared.

'Don't fool around like a ventriloquist's dummy,' the fair-haired man said in a high, petulant voice. 'Get this door open.'

The head announced that there had been a bomb scare; the staff had been given fifteen minutes to clear the premises, so it was not possible to admit customers.

This was greeted with a storm of protests about cash needed for last-minute Christmas purchases and the necessity of paying in takings. 'Barclaycard won't be pleased,' one man said. 'I'm not going to pay interest just because you haven't passed on my cheque.'

The head was withdrawn and after a few moments was replaced by the whole body of another man, chunky, leather-jacketed. He closed the door behind him and leant against it, in the manner of a sheriff keeping a lynch mob at bay.

The fair-haired man said, 'May I introduce myself? I am Terence Palmer, one of your customers. You have my money. I have a long journey to make. Although you may not have noticed it, the weather is worsening by the minute and it is imperative that I start soon.'

The young man said, 'On your bike, then.'

'I shall report you to the manager.'

'You do that.'

'Safeways had a scare last week,' a woman said. 'We had to stand around in the rain for over an hour and then they didn't find anything.'

'Who would want to do a thing like this on Christmas Eve?' an old man asked Terence.

53

'Someone from the Nat West, perhaps?'

A man in a blue raincoat pushed through the crowd and was immediately admitted by the leather-jacketed sentry.

'He the bomb squad?' a woman asked.

'No, local CID. He come round when our shop was burgled. They won't call the bomb squad 'less they find a package.'

Terence, who was short, stood on tiptoe to peer through the nearest window. The staff were assembled at the far end of the foyer, looking bored and irresolute. The man in the blue raincoat had disappeared and there seemed to be little activity.

'They catch them? The blokes what done your shop?'

'No. Just brought back a lot of empty bottles. "What's this for?" I asked. "Don't you have a dustbin at the police station?"'

A queue had formed in front of the cash dispenser. Terence joined the queue, reflecting grimly that it would be much longer by the time he had finished. He was never able to remember his pin number; he knew that there were two sevens, a four and a one, but had difficulty assembling them in the right order. Today, the machine was out of patience; by the time he had tried three combinations, it told him to see the manager and confiscated his card. Terence thumped the machine. It had begun to snow heavily.

'College lecturer arrested trying to break

into cash dispenser,' an amused voice said at his elbow.

Terence turned to see one of the administrative staff from the training college smiling archly at him.

'Darling Jenny!'

'Amanda, actually.'

'Gorgeous, heaven-sent Amanda, have you any money?'

'I will have, if you haven't damaged the machine.'

'Could you be so full of Christmas goodwill as to get fifty pounds for me? I haven't enough petrol and by now I should be half-way to this God-forsaken place where I'm spending the festive season.'

'Fifty pounds for petrol? Where can you be going?'

'There may be extras, like finding accommodation if I get stuck on the way, which seems more likely with every minute that passes.'

She inserted her card and tapped away efficiently. 'There you are. Have a lovely Christmas.' She handed him the money and murmured, 'I may ask for interest.'

'There is no way I'll have a lovely Christmas. Not with Anita's mother around.' Snow was trickling down his neck and he felt the familiar onset of self-pity. 'She's one of those women who can never leave any object or person as she finds it. If you're sitting quietly reading, she plumps herself down beside you and says, "Don't put your book down, Terence, I don't want to stop you reading," and prattles on for the next half-hour. If you're up and doing, it's, "Working, Terence? This I don't believe." Last Christmas I got a shock changing a light bulb, thanks to her.'

'Poor Terence.'

'It will be like spending Christmas with a human sheep-dog constantly snapping at your ankles.'

'What about the rest of the family?'

'Anita actually enjoys wrangling with her mother. Nicholas—the brother—will only be with us in his bodily manifestation; his spirit will be roaming free in some desert region. The father is dying.'

'Really dying?'

'Yes, yes, people do, you know. They really do shuffle off this mortal coil. Anita and her mother and Nicholas are unable to accept this—but it does happen. In fact, knowing this family, it will probably happen on Christmas Day.'

'Well, at least Anita will have you to comfort her.' Her voice had become tart. Terence, watching her walk away, reflected on the general absence of charity.

*   *   *

56

Florence and Anita were working together in the kitchen. Florence sat upright on a stool, back straight, the great shelf of her breast creating the illusion of a flat stomach. She had long ago decided that attention to posture was essential for a fat woman. One must be thrusting, positive, never a suggestion of apology; every movement, the smallest gesture, must be executed with the precise perfection of the ballerina, and, above all, the head must be held high. This had now become so natural to her that she had no idea of the studied elegance with which she cracked another egg. Anita, unable and unwilling to compete with her mother's vitality, was content to present a picture of languid abandon, her face lemon pale beneath the brilliant hair, her limbs seemingly reluctant to meet the small demands made on them. 'I think I must have been a slave in one of my earlier existences.'

'I doubt that your owner got much out of you.'

'There were slaves and slaves. I wouldn't have been the willing kind. A little bit of smouldering, I think, would have suited me. You do realise you're using all the eggs?'

'Nicholas is bringing a further supply. Sophia says there's never any difficulty getting eggs hereabouts.'

'And particularly not now when they come with a health warning.'

57

'I'm not scrambling them. Egg nog can't hurt anyone.'

'On the contrary, uncooked egg is about the worst thing...'

'People will want a nice warming drink which they can have without worrying about driving.'

'Adding eggs and cream to whisky doesn't make it any less potent.'

'It neutralises the effect,' Florence said with cheerful firmness.

'At the end of this party, those who aren't laid low with salmonella will be arrested for driving while under the influence.'

They continued in this vein for some time, neither taking the other seriously; instances of real bad feeling were rare between them. Florence worked quickly and untidily, dropping eggshells on to the table and occasionally the floor. She shouted instructions to Anita, who obeyed at her leisure. 'Cut the French bread into pieces—even you can do that at a reasonable speed. Then you can cut the cheeses.'

'What's wrong with letting them help themselves to cheese?'

'They'd make pigs of themselves. The last party I gave at home, one man ate all the Brie.'

'If the egg doesn't do for them, the Brie will,' Anita said, cutting the French bread.

Florence poured the last of the egg nog

58

into a cracked earthenware jug of some antiquity. 'Perhaps we shouldn't have any of this; just keep it for the visitors. We'll serve it out here, then they needn't see where it's come from.'

'It does look rather like one of those pots people dig up on archaeological expeditions, doesn't it?'

Florence rubbed her hands down her thighs to dry them. 'We'll have coffee now, shall we?'

'What is Sophia doing while we're wrecking her kitchen?'

'She's sitting with your father.'

'Shouldn't you be doing that?'

'One thing about an Aga, it does keep things beautifully warm.' Florence poured coffee.

'I said...'

'Yes, I heard what you said. He's asleep.' She sat on a stool and looked out of the window as she sipped the coffee. 'It's beginning to snow again. I hope Nicholas will come straight back. It would be just like him to waste time playing games with this child—what's his name?'

'Andrew. I don't think he's a playful child.'

'Difficult, is he? She'll have to be firm with him. Is she firm with him, this Frances?'

Anita piled bread into two wicker baskets which Florence had lined with kitchen paper

59

in the interests of hygiene. 'He needs a sense of security rather than firmness.'

'Those mince pies should be done now. Just take a look and if they're done, put them in the bottom oven to keep warm.' She began to roll out pastry. 'I think I'll make a lemon curd tart for us to have after they've gone. I do so love lemon curd.' She kept looking out of the window at the swirling snow as she worked. 'He will never feel secure if she isn't firm with him. A boy needs to have his boundaries clearly marked.'

'I would have thought ...' Anita said, gazing dubiously at the mince pies.

'Oh yes, you would think. Think is all you ever do. Whereas I know. It's an instinct a mother has.' She placed a hand on the lower region of her stomach, leaving a floury imprint which Anita thought looked mildly obscene.

'Are these done?'

'Of course they're done. I can't think what sort of food you and Terence have if you can't even tell whether mince pies are done. Do as I told you and put them in the bottom oven.' She made a neat circle of pastry and laid it in a flan ring. 'One has to be very firm with boys. I recall vividly when Nicholas was young, we were walking in Gunnersbury Park. I had you in a pushchair. It was snowing and difficult to see. He wanted to go off on his sled down to the pond where some boys were skating. Of course, I wouldn't let him go. He got into a rage that was quite out of all proportion. You know the way a boy can blow himself up fit to burst over something totally unimportant.'

'His freedom, for example?' Anita, elbows on table, one hand supporting her averted face, was listening intently now.

'Freedom? Aged six?' Florence ladled lemon curd into the tart and placed it in the oven. 'Self-will. I could see this was a confrontation I could not afford to lose. I let go of you and managed to grab the sled. He fought quite violently, screaming, "I have to, I have to!" "There's only one 'have to' I know anything about," I said. I bent down to unbutton his trousers and he hit me on the nose. He had a fistful of snow and there must have been a stone in it. There was blood everywhere and you rocking about in the pushchair as though you meant to tip it over, and both of you screaming.' She looked at her most voluptuous, eyes shining and mouth curved in pleasure, savouring her victory as if it were edible. 'We didn't have any nonsense about skating on the pond after that. It sobered him.'

'It must have been very frightening for him.' Anita was sobered too. 'He probably thought he'd done you a terrible injury.'

'It would have been far more frightening if he had had his own way. You can never

61

afford to lose a battle with a child.'

'It had to be a battle? It didn't occur to you to say, "Yes, Nicholas, we'll all go down to the pond"?'

'He wanted to go on his own. I could see it in his face, he meant to get away from me.'

'It probably had all sorts of sexual overtones, too—blood and snow.'

Florence began to clean the worktop vigorously, shooting more eggshells on to the floor. 'Spare us the psychology.'

'You emasculated him.'

'How popular you must be with your clients.'

'Psychology isn't about being popular.'

'More's the pity. It would be a great deal more successful if it were.'

'And I still like you—God knows why.' Anita hunched forward, clawing her hair into a ravelled mat which covered her face while she brooded on the matter.

'That's very unhygienic.'

'I suppose it's because you are so irrepressible.' Anita sounded distanced by concealment. 'It really takes something to go through life being so completely wrong-headed and never coming to grief.'

Florence's face suddenly crumpled. 'How can you talk about grief at a time like this?'

'I would have thought it was an appropriate time.'

There was silence between them,

something neither felt comfortable about. Florence took a piece of kitchen paper and dabbed her cheeks, although there was no trace of tears. Anita found a broom and began to sweep the floor.

'You'll have to use a mop,' Florence said. She cupped her face in her hands, meditating. 'I suppose you could say my life has been a series of unpleasant surprises,' she said, looking like someone who has ridden every crisis in her life with verve. 'I married a man who seemed to have a great future ahead of him and let it slip out of his hands. My extremely gifted children failed to use their talents. None of my nearest and dearest has fulfilled their potential, they've all turned away from rather than towards. It's a part of the age, I suppose, this extraordinary dissatisfaction people have, this passion for rejection. Where, I ask myself, does it all lead?'

Anita, on her knees mopping, said, 'That's a rhetorical question, I assume. The last thing you usually want is an answer.'

Florence tossed another eggshell on to the pile on the floor. 'You know those films where the man rides off over the crest of the hill and one isn't encouraged to enquire what happened to him on the other side; or there's the character who walks away with a radiant face into a new life; or, in the theatre, someone says as the curtain comes down,

'"Things will never be the same again." Well, I always feel that's where I came in. And I know why they never take the story any further. It's so dull.'

'I wouldn't have said your life has been exactly dull,' Anita said, a captious Cinderella resting on her haunches.

'You're too young to know what it was like at first. I expected it to be a marvellously exciting time.'

'You have had quite a few marvellously exciting times, though not always with Father.'

'One must take what opportunities come one's way.'

'You've certainly done that.'

'If I'd had important things to do, it would have been different.'

'I wouldn't have said that sex was something you turned to in the absence of worthwhile activities. As far as you're concerned, worthwhile activities are things you do to keep your mind off the really important business of sex.'

'You have no idea how frustrating my life has been. Had your father gone into the diplomatic service...'

'We shouldn't have had over forty years of peace if you'd been on the diplomatic circuit.'

'I don't think you should speak to me like that, Anita.'

'As one of the unpleasant surprises of your life, I feel I should have the right of reply. All I ever heard in my childhood was what you expected—from me, from Nicholas, from my father. I don't think you once took a really good look at any of us. Perhaps things might not have been so disappointing for you if you'd inspected what was on offer.'

Florence said, as though appealing to some unseen presence out in the snow, 'All my life I have been fighting this tendency to let go. I have been the one who has held things together. No one has any idea of the strain I have had to bear.'

'Why not let go yourself and see what happens?'

'But I never gave up in spite of the strain. I meant life to be good and positive and I held on.' She turned a glowing face to Anita. 'Do you know what Great Aunt Edith said to me not long before she died? "I marvel at you, Florence," she said. "You are Bronze Age woman. You were born too late to have known a Golden Age, so you set yourself to construct out of what material was available to you, a goodish Bronze Age." I'm not sure what she meant, but it was the nicest thing she ever said to me.'

'Sod Great Aunt Edith.'

'I think we'd better go and change now. I seem to have made rather a mess of this skirt.'

'You haven't taken in anything I've said, have you?'

'Fortunately not.' She went into the hall and Anita could hear her singing 'The holly and the ivy' as she went up the stairs.

*   *   *

'So many people,' Konrad said.

Florence, who had replaced Sophia by his bedside, said, 'Not yet. They haven't arrived yet.'

He was thinking not of the people who would visit the cottage this morning, but of the large cast contained in his own house—the refugee, the husband, father, painter, lover. Too many at this stage of his life. A drastic reduction was necessary, a calling-in of all these people flitting in and out of his house, cluttering up his mind and consuming far too much energy.

'We had to arrange a little party,' Florence said. 'For the sake of the young people. They expect something at Christmas. You do understand, don't you?'

He lay still, meditating on what her words really meant. It had been like this over the years, the quiet withdrawal which always preceded a response. Who could have known the frantic person rushing hither and thither within him, probing this possibility, discarding that, searching desperately in

66

another corner of the mind before the calm answer was vouchsafed? Always the inside and outside person so at variance. All he had learnt to do in sixty years was impose a certain discipline of presentation, refuse to allow chaos to predominate.

'You mustn't reproach yourself, Florence.' He was pleased to have decoded her meaning. 'There is nothing for which you should reproach yourself.'

'I wasn't reproaching myself.' She loomed over him, flushed and agitated. 'It's you who should reproach yourself, giving way like this, refusing treatment. "Do not go gentle into that good night ..."'

He smiled, a dubious enterprise in his condition. The grimace momentarily fragmented his face and reassembled it in the likeness of one of the more licentious Roman gods, spewing fountains of mirth.

'I shall never go anywhere gently, Florence—I am a blunderer. But I shan't rage either. I have never raged and I'm not going to start now.'

It was the longest and firmest statement he had made for some time and it exhausted them both. Florence fussed with his pillows and poured a glass of water from the jug on the bedside table.

'I'll come back and tell you all about the party,' she said as she left the room.

It transpired that Frances had very little to do in the way of shopping.

'Thomas did quite a lot for me yesterday,' she said. 'And on Christmas Day we're all coming to Sophia—did she tell you?'

'No, I don't think she mentioned it.' Nicholas put the gear into reverse, his expression thoughtful. 'Would Andrew have liked a ride?' he asked as he turned the car away from the house.

'I didn't ask him. I wanted an opportunity to talk to you.' She spoke with the disconcerting straightforwardness of a child.

Nicholas drove the car on to the forest path with great care, reassessing his part in the setting up of this expedition.

'I've been thinking about this ever since Sophia said you were coming. You don't mind, do you?'

He stopped the car and looked at her, not quite sure what it was she might have been anticipating. A brightly coloured scarf swathed head and shoulders and the glimpse he had of her face did little to set his mind at rest. How many times in bazaars had he seen the face turned briefly to regard him with that intense curiosity which the stranger arouses? Only these eyes were not dark, they were like clear water and seemed to reflect back at him his own unease. What had he

68

anticipated when he so uncharacteristically suggested this trip?

'I'm not a great talker,' he said.

'I don't mean chit-chat.'

He decided to treat her as an enthusiastic schoolgirl. 'Well, then—where and when? Here, in the car, before we do the shopping, or afterwards?'

'Oh no. There are so many things I've wanted to ask you. I heard you on the radio.' She seemed to consider this a sufficient explanation.

'I don't quite see how ...' he mused. Nicholas musing always had the look of someone unlikely to arrive at a conclusion. Others besides Frances had thought what mountain winds and desert suns had honed and hollowed that face and faded the searching eyes. A man whom distant horizons called could scarcely be expected to turn his mind to the how and where of domestic intimacy.

'Look, it's nine o'clock now,' Frances said. 'We have plenty of time. We could stop on the way. I'm looking after the house of some friends while they're away and I have to make sure the heating comes on and all that. I could make you some coffee.' Again, there was something childish in her assumption of authority.

He screwed up his eyes, peering ahead. It was snowing hard and the visibility was poor.

69

'I don't want to miss the turning on to the road.'

'Don't you want to stop at the house? You haven't said.'

'I hadn't realised I was expected to show initiative.' He was aware of sounding as touchy as a Ranger Scout whose seniority has been challenged.

She did not speak again until they came to the road, when she said hesitantly, 'You turn left, in case you didn't realise ... I mean, I don't know whether you've been to the town before; but then I expect you looked at the map before you set off.' Out of the corner of his eye he had a glimpse of lowered lids and puckered mouth.

'I'm sorry. I didn't mean to upset you.'

'Oh no, I'm the one—to be sorry, I mean. I shouldn't have assumed...'

They drove silently into the town. Florence had given Nicholas a long list and it took an hour to fulfil all her commissions. The sky had cleared and the sun was shining, making the snow so much heaped sugar, when at last they returned to the car.

'Now,' Nicholas said. 'Direct me to this house.'

'If you're sure...'

'We have to check the heating, don't we, whatever else.'

They were silent again, their minds occupied by that whatever else.

70

The house was on the edge of the forest, not far from the turning to the track which led eventually to Sophia's cottage; it glinted and sparkled in its white raiment. At one of the windows a Christmas tree, bedecked with shiny balls of green and red and gold, spoke of goodwill, although its main purpose was as a sign of occupancy. Frances and Nicholas sat gazing at the house for some moments before getting out of the car. It looked as if it was contained in one of those glass globes which when shaken produce a picturesque semblance of snowfall. Neither was quite sure how they had arrived here, let alone why. If they had had more time it might have been different. Tomorrow, however, was not another day, tomorrow was Christmas Day and then there was Boxing Day and after that the workaday world would assert its hold. Nicholas got out of the car and walked up the short drive. The snow came up to Frances's knees as she followed him. She found the key and they entered the house. It was small and gave the impression of comfort in spite of the intense cold; the drawing-room had been left a little untidy with books lying around and suggested a friendly confidence in the temporary steward. Nicholas and Frances hesitated, looking in from the hall. She said, 'You must think me very silly, bringing you here like this.'

'Not at all.' He propelled her gently over to the low settee. 'Though I'm not sure what it is we have to talk about.'

She looked at him, surprised he should fail to understand, as though they had already been in communication on the matter. 'Your travels, of course. Why you do it—all the hardship, the living on the fringes of civilisation, experiencing life on the margins of existence.'

'Oh dear, that sounds very like a quote.'

'Yes, of course it was a quote. I told you I listened to that radio programme.'

'You take things too seriously,' he admonished.

'But you're a serious person.' The grey eyes would accept no denial. 'I've read your book about your travels in India three times. You ask some very serious questions in it—about Western materialism and the worship of technology, the value we place on money and possessions. You said about books that people here aren't interested in their content, only in how much money they make and whether the author uses a word processor.'

Nicholas shrugged. 'That sort of comment is one of the side-effects of the India experience.'

'But it went much deeper with you, surely?' She had taken off her anorak and now paused, arms upraised to remove the scarf. 'When I read your book I was sure you would end up living in India. Why didn't you?'

She seated herself, knees drawn together, hands clasped above them, and waited for Nicholas to collect his thoughts, unaware that she had outraged him by this direct questioning of his motives. In his view there was a certain territory sacred to each individual and to trespass would be like breaking a taboo—terrible things might come to pass. He realised, however, that to make too much of this might invite further penetration, so he seated himself beside her and said, in the tone he might have adopted had he been giving a lecture, 'The Indians seem to me still to be living in a subconscious dream that I'd like to share, but can't because I'm too wide awake. When people become fully conscious they go mad; like those unfortunates who win the pools, they can only think of getting as many of the goodies within their grasp as possible. That seems to me what has happened to Western society.'

'You didn't feel you wanted to become like the old men by the Ganges who have given up all possessions?'

'No, I just found myself wondering if it would work so well in a cold climate.'

She studied him, head to one side, eyebrows raised, conveying the most maddening impression that she knew his reasons better than he did himself. He said, 'I'm sorry to disillusion you, but all my experiences so far have shown me alternative ways of life which I can admire but not become a part of.'

The coloured lights of the Christmas tree were reflected on the glaring white of the wall opposite. Beyond the window a robin sang. Frances said wryly, 'Whereas what happens to most people is they become part of something first and only think about it afterwards.'

Now that her interest was withdrawn from him, it was as if a light had been switched off. Her face was sullen, absorbed in some grief of her own. He found himself impelled by the curiosity he had felt when he first saw her, a need not so much to find the answer to a riddle as to touch something in her. Perhaps, just to touch. 'How did you get yourself into this housekeeping situation?' he asked.

She looked at him, gravely considering whether to answer or not, and then looked away. Intimacy came of that pause.

'I developed a passion for Jonathan, my sister's husband—it's something younger sisters are prone to.' She told him this as though presenting him with a small confidence. He was aware that she was warmed by his interest. 'He was sensitive

74

and artistic, you know the sort of thing, a combination of Keats and Rupert Brooke, with the look of not being long for this harsh world. I thought that quite proper. I was into CND and thought the nuclear winter was just round the corner and that anyone who looked fit and played rugby was beyond bearing.' She was discovering that it was possible to laugh at herself. Nicholas wondered how it had come about that he had behaved in this intrusive fashion, he who had a horror of inviting confidences. 'Then, when it all fell apart—you know that my sister left him?—I desperately wanted to help. I saw quite a lot of Jonathan. He and Andrew were staying down here with Thomas and Margery. It was a happy time for me. We used to go for long walks and talk about the pointlessness of existence. I didn't realise he really meant it.' Nicholas, by now acutely uncomfortable, was seeking a means of retreat. Frances said, 'After he shot himself, I felt terribly guilty—not just because of my sister, but because I had known how he felt and hadn't understood. For a time, I believed it was I who had killed him. I stayed with Thomas and Margery most weekends. They were marvellous. When Margery died I felt I had to do all I could to help.'

She looked at him and smiled. 'So, now you know.' The room had begun to darken.

Beyond the window the sky looked sick against the whiteness of snow. Nicholas said curtly, 'A bit over-dramatic, surely, and a very rash decision.'

As if his hand had smashed the smile from her face, she jerked her head to one side. No conventional words of sympathy could so have strengthened the feeling between them. 'There was nothing to decide.' She dismissed his questioning of her motives with scorn. 'Thomas and Margery treated me as a daughter; when Margery died I took the daughter's role.'

'A little unusual nowadays—I doubt that Anita would see it as her role to give up her way of life in order to care for my mother.'

'I don't know about your sister.' She reacted with a flash of resentment. 'I didn't have a way of life to give up. My father died when I was five and my mother when I was twelve. My sister and I were sent to boarding school and farmed out for the holidays. It didn't make sense to me when people talked about the need to break away from the family—I was desperate for a family.'

'Even so, it's not a very satisfactory situation to have got yourself into.' He tried to sound indifferent but it was too late; the tension between them increased with each word spoken. 'Isn't it time you gave some thought to it?'

'Why have I been talking to you about

this? You don't begin ...' She pounded fist on breastbone. 'I don't think, I feel. Can you understand that? I feel how it would be for Andrew were he to go to boarding school. I feel Thomas's humiliation, unable to care for his grandson. No amount of thinking can cancel out their pain.'

'All very worthy, no doubt, but some thought—'

'Where has thinking got you?' She flushed crimson and turned away. 'I'm sorry. But you're not a very good example, are you?' She got up and went to the window.

'Example of what?' He was on his feet, shouting at her. The room was almost dark now and snow was massing against the window-ledge. She said, 'It's snowing again. It's time we were on our way.' An authoritative young person once more.

He took her by the shoulders and turned her to face him. 'Answer me.'

'I can't. I don't know why I said that. You remind me of Andrew. He needs a shield, so he has glasses he can hide behind.'

'Is this supposed to make sense?'

'You have an invisible shield, haven't you? You have these wonderful experiences, but when you write or talk about them you never actually tell anything important about yourself.'

'There is nothing to tell. I happen to be one of those people who feel most fully alive when life is stripped of all the trappings.' He had said this before and it seemed to state his position well enough; the only concern the statement afforded him was his willingness to repeat it.

'So what happens?' she asked eagerly. 'That's what I've wanted to ask you ever since I heard you on the radio. You have this great experience of coming fully alive, but what does it lead to?'

'It doesn't have to lead anywhere. I'm not a missionary, I'm a natural nomad.'

'But no one undergoes the kind of hardship you've experienced if there isn't anything in it for themselves.' She moved closer to him, her eyes intent on reading his face. 'There must be something you hope to find. That's what I wanted—to know what your hope is.'

There was just enough light to see the ivory oval of her face blur as he bent to kiss her. She gave a little gasp and he felt a tremor run down her body. Her lips, cheek, the tip of her nose and hollow of her throat, were stingingly cold to his lips. She must have stepped back against something—a stool, perhaps, it was too dark to see. She stumbled. When he steadied her she stood before him, immobile. He found her anorak and held it out for her, but she was unable to get her stiff arms into it without his help.

'You're a block of ice,' he said, and

drawing her down on to the window-seat he began to chafe the helpless hands. Her face, in the snow light, was bloodless, but he saw that a single tear glistened on her cheek like a pearl on wax.

*   *   *

Once they were outside the house, the snow fully occupied their attention. Conditions had deteriorated considerably during the time they had been talking. Nicholas, who had experienced a few life and death situations, had never felt so apprehensive as now, faced with the possibility that he might have to explain to his mother how it came about that the provisions she needed must be fetched by sled (always supposing Sophia had such a thing) from a car which was stranded outside a house where it had had no reason to stand for any longer than it took to adjust a central heating switch. In the twenty minutes it took to dig the car free he lost more energy due to sheer panic than physical effort.

After he had dropped Frances at her house, he was not sorry that his progress to Sophia's cottage was necessarily slow. He needed time to think. He had for many years been without that kind of anxiety which springs from close involvement in the lives of others. He had always made sure that he could slide gently out of relationships whenever it suited him. He had been free to avoid demands and to turn from questions he did not wish to consider and thoughts he did not wish to entertain. To some extent, this freedom had depended on the few fixtures in his life remaining constant. His father's illness had disturbed this stability. There were questions it might not be possible to avoid, such as what was to become of his mother. It was hardly to be hoped that she would fail to raise the matter. He felt threatened, aware that impending change might necessitate a re-examination of his life.

*   *   *

Florence stood staring out of the sitting-room window, eyes wide and unblinking as if hypnotised. She wore a red tartan kilt and waistcoat and a frilly white blouse.

Anita said, 'You look like a Scottish noblewoman who has been forced to take refuge in a croft.'

Florence patted her bosom, not dissatisfied with this description. 'When does a snowstorm become a blizzard?'

'It's a blizzard when there is a high wind and the snow goes racing past the window slantwise and builds up into huge drifts in which cars have to be abandoned and farmers have to go out digging up sheep and villages are cut off and food supplies run out and...'

'I get the idea, thank you.'

'And, worst of all, telly goes off the air.'

The wind howled in the chimney and one of the logs spat and crackled. Tobias, who had been conducting an exhaustive examination of his claws, started back, hissing.

'You don't think Nicholas has gone off to help some farmer dig up sheep?' Florence asked uneasily.

Anita kicked at a spark which was singeing the rug. 'There aren't many farms hereabouts. I expect he's building a neat little igloo for himself and Frances.'

Florence frowned, finding this image displeasing. She rubbed at the window-pane with a tissue, but it was clotted with snow from the outside and the visibility remained poor. Another cause of displeasure came to her mind. 'And what can have happened to Terence? You don't seem very concerned about him.'

'If Terence were caught in a blizzard in the middle of the Steppes he would happen across the only shelter available in a thousand miles.'

'It's half-past eleven. Where can Nicholas be?'

'More to the point, where is Sophia? She should be here ready to greet all the eager early arrivals.'

'She's out fetching more logs.'

'I'll go and help her.'

'You will do *what*?' Florence transferred her attention from the snow to her daughter. 'Since when have you become one of the hewers of wood and drawers of water?'

'I'm going to carry, not hew.'

'It won't do much for that dress.'

'There's a dreadful old duffel coat hanging up in the scullery; I'll put that on.'

'You should have worn something more flouncy; that dress makes you look all skin and bone.' She was speaking to herself, Anita had gone. Another gust of wind sent the candles on the mantelshelf flickering wildly and two Christmas cards fell from the window-ledge. 'I don't know about you,' Florence was driven to conversing with Tobias, 'but I hate anything taken to excess. This is definitely too much.' He opened his mouth wide, revealing pink roof vaulting and a number of sharp white teeth.

Anita, wrapped in the duffel coat and stumbling in boots too large for her, had difficulty orientating herself once out of the back door. The snow was blinding and the wind nearly pulled her off her feet; twigs and branches whirled past her and while she stood clutching at the drainpipe a cloth torn from a clothes line wrapped itself round her face. She fought her way along the side of the house, recalling stories of people who had died in snow only a few hundred yards from a cottage door. Fortunately, once away from the cottage, a low hedge and a line of straggling bushes provided hand-holds as well as marking the way.

The wood was stored in a compartment at the far end of the long shed where Sophia slept. When she reached the building Anita peered through a crack at the side of the window, hoping to get a glimpse of the interior. The curtains were still drawn and she was convinced the room contained a secret; but there was nothing to be seen, and even had there been her eyes were watering so much it was doubtful whether she would have obtained a very clear picture. As she clawed her way along the side of the building she wondered what Sophia used the place for normally; it was quite large and would have made a good workroom, but her mother had said that Sophia now worked at a craft centre on the outskirts of the town.

In the wood store logs were piled almost to the roof and Sophia was perched on a pair of steps.

'I keep a small pile for immediate use,' she said as Anita joined her, 'but it's dwindled to nothing.' She began to hand down logs. 'We can put them on that sled and a sack of coal as well. I loving pulling a sled, don't you?'

'I prefer being pulled.'

A hurricane lamp swayed wildly from a rafter and Anita could barely distinguish the sled among the leaping shadows. She began to stack the logs in the wicker baskets which Sophia had brought with her. 'Where's the coal?' She could imagine her dress being filthy before the party started. It was Terence's favourite—a shimmering emerald sheath—and she had worn it in the hope of appeasing him when he eventually arrived.

'In the lean-to at the back of this store. We shall have to do a little digging, I'm afraid; the snow has blocked the entrance.'

In the event, it was Sophia who did the digging while Anita hauled out the sled and began to stack the laden wicker baskets on it, tipping one and scrabbling after the logs in the snow. Anita worked moodily, Sophia with zest. Sophia, black-velvet trousers and brocaded jacket muffled by an old trench coat, and wearing a black beret, was a different and decidedly more rakish person than the Sophia of yesterday. A witch with carnal attributes, Anita thought, imagining that playful jester's smile directed at a man. She was suddenly quite sure that once there had been a man in her place, helping to heft logs, and that he and Sophia would have laughed quite a lot as they worked. Almost, she caught the sound of his laughter.

84

'You're like my mother,' she said, surprised.

'We are sisters.'

'You both have an appetite for pleasure.'

Sophia rested from her spadework to look in Anita's direction, more as an aid to hearing than sight. 'What happened to the daughter, then?'

'My mother is too big for me. She dwarfs everyone around her—except my father,' Anita shouted into the wind. 'There's never any peace where she is, nowhere that I can feel I am me. All my childhood I had to stay clenched tight, ready to parry thrusts from my mother.'

Even now, in order to talk to Sophia alone, she had been driven to making a goodwill gesture in a blizzard. Sophia seemed to understand something of this, for when they had heaved the sack of coal on to the sled, she covered it with an old tarpaulin sheet. 'This can wait for a few moments. Come back into the wood shed.'

Anita, huddled in the duffel coat, teeth chattering, was determined to take her opportunity.

'You say Florence dwarfed everyone except your father,' Sophia said. 'So what about him?'

'I adored him when I was very young. His stories were stranger and more exciting than any in my books.' Since she arrived here

85

those stories had been coming back to her and now, in spite of physical misery, she recalled what an adventure a snowstorm had been in his company. 'My sled became a troika and I heard the jingle of harness; I was hurled down great slopes, past tall, pointed trees with stars in their branches, towards a silver sheen of frozen water. And such a race of blood in the veins I nearly burst with expectancy! He never had to make an effort to get on my level, the childhood world seemed real to him. God was real, too—more real than some of His human creatures. He used to say Christ stood the world on its head. I think my father was at home with the upside-down view.'

The shed door swung open, buffeted by the wind, and Anita clutched Sophia's arm, afraid she might be distracted and move away while there were things yet to be said. 'Then, when I got older, I saw that he was quite different from my friends' fathers, who all had faces smooth as putty and used their features sparingly, while my daddy popped his eyes and showed his back teeth when he talked, and laughed from his belly. I could see some of my friends were quite alarmed by him. First of all this confused me and then it embarrassed me. I wanted a daddy who was bland like all the others. I left him behind like a child I had grown too old to play with. It never seemed possible to find him again, later, when I wanted to. There wasn't the space. If you left any space in our house my mother occupied it, just as she fills any gap in conversation.'

'Yet you found the space when you were young.'

'But I can't find my way back to where I was then.' She clutched Sophia's arm more tightly, shouting above the noise of the wind. 'He's going to die, Sophia; I'm so afraid he's going to die now when I'm beginning to discover how much I need him.' She had lost all restraint.

'Help me, Sophia; I need someone to help me so much.' She flung the words out like a prayer and Sophia put her arms around her.

'Anita, my love, your father is dying.'

'I know, that's what I said.'

'Not quite.'

But Anita had exhausted herself and was not listening. She was comforted by Sophia's embrace and felt her prayer had been answered.

As they were hauling the sled down the garden, Nicholas arrived. 'Just what I need,' he said. 'I'll see to this for you and then I'll load it with Mother's comestibles.' He hoped that by performing this double service he would restore himself to his mother's favour. Florence, who had become increasingly agitated while left on her own, took his arrival as a good omen and was not disposed to criticise.

When she arrived, Florence had thought the forest denuded of people; looking from her bedroom window that night and seeing the garden bathed in cold blue light, the white, hooded trees standing around, she had felt she had come to one of those secret places to which bad fairies lure innocent travellers. It was possible to believe in wolves and bears, witches and wizards, more easily than in other human beings. This was not the place she had loved as a child.

Today, as the blizzard raged, she had even been visited by the notion that there were no other people anywhere. Some great catastrophe had struck England, if not Planet Earth, and of humankind only a remnant survived here in this cottage.

It was surprising, therefore, to discover that so many forest creatures had tunnelled out of burrows, setts or forms. Watching their arrival from the cottage doorway, it was indeed difficult to tell what manner of thing was emerging from the shadow of the trees; and even as they made their way down the path, badgers, beavers and rabbits came as readily to mind as any other creature. It was only when woolly hats and scarves, blankets, sheepskin coats, ponchos and parkas, boots and Wellingtons had been stripped away and deposited in a mountainous heap in the scullery, that they were revealed as more or less human, though there were one or two goblins and gnomes among them and one satyr. It was apparent to Florence that Sophia's invitations had been sent without tact or discrimination to near neighbours, some of whom might well be living in charcoal burners' huts.

The people of the kind for whom Florence had made her preparations appeared to accept the presence of the ruder forest dwellers with equanimity, indeed seemed on conversational terms with them. Several gathered round a mauve-faced bundle of bones with a cough like heavy artillery fire, commenting with every semblance of sincerity on how much improved she was. The old satyr had an immediate audience for gossip of a scabrous nature about a man renowned for his campaign for the preservation of the forest, whom Florence had hoped might be among those invited.

''Course 'e won't stand for no encroachment. Don't want anyone else springing o' 'is traps, do 'e?'

'Up to his old tricks again?' This from a man who had emerged sleek and pearly grey from his storm wrappings; a man to whom Florence would unhesitatingly have entrusted her legal affairs.

'Mary Plunkett.'

The satyr's listeners considered Mary Plunkett as if tasting her ripeness. A dishevelled old crone, who smelt of urine and leaf mould, asked, 'Where you 'ear that, then, Jem?'

' 'Eared it and see'd it.'

Florence said to a reasonably refined-looking woman who was standing on the fringe of this group, 'I hope no one from the Plunkett family is here?'

'Particularly not Mary, by the look of her—else there'll be a baby in the crib this Christmas Eve.'

Florence gave her a glass of egg nog, which she was pressing on people she did not much take to. The whisky she held in reserve. The rustics were mostly content with ale, although she had an idea the satyr had his eye on the whisky bottle.

Florence prowled around, looking first in one room, then another. The herding instinct was very strong in her. 'There are far too many people squashed into the hall while the sitting-room is half-empty,' she reported to Sophia, whom she found sitting on the stairs, comforting Tobias.

'What fools these mortals be,' Sophia whispered in Tobias's ear. She seemed to think the disposal of her guests to be no concern of hers. In her jaunty beret and velvet brocaded jumper suit she was more

Florence's idea of Dick Whittington than a hostess at a formal, adult party.

'And there are some very odd people here,' Florence persisted. 'I suppose they were all invited.'

'I shouldn't think there would be many chance passersby today,' Sophia answered indifferently.

'It's going to be very difficult for people to get to the toilet in this crush. I only hope they're all continent.'

'There might be the odd near miss, I suppose.'

'You do this deliberately,' Florence said, feeling about fourteen. 'You always have had an irresistible desire to break up any sign of conformity.'

'Incontinence is an infirmity not a lack of conformity.'

'You set up a conventional social occasion, like a Christmas party, then proceed to wreck it.'

Sophia, a provocative elfin child again, tickled Tobias behind the ear. 'She set it up, didn't she? T'weren't us. That lady set it up.'

'You provided the people.'

'They are my neighbours; they provided themselves.'

There was knocking on the front door and Florence turned, her kilt swinging as she moved. Tobias stretched a lazy paw and pulled several threads from the seat as she walked away.

The new arrivals were a Mr. and Mrs. Prentice, who seemed much aggrieved at having been asked out on such a morning and firmly of the opinion that the snow had been sent particularly to annoy them. 'Something awful always happens to us at Christmas,' Mrs. Prentice declared, including Florence's imposing figure in the present calamity. 'You look splendid, I must say, but then you haven't had to go out today.'

By the time Florence had divested the Prentices of their protective layers, the party had formed into groups. What Florence persisted in calling the crudities were still in possession of the hall; those whom she designated artisans (the man who delivered Sophia's logs, a jobbing builder and two motor mechanics) had moved into the dining-room and were working their way steadily through the cheeses uninhibited by Anita's attempts to cube and strip; the professional people were in the sitting-room, talking knowledgeably about the economic situation and obviously one step ahead of the Chancellor. Florence, who found the conversation of professional people lacking in spice, regretted the absence of members of the business community.

Nicholas was out in the garden playing with the child, Andrew, and two young women, one of whom was presumably Frances. Two toddlers of indeterminate sex were watching them and crying in a desultory way. Anita was moving from room to room, peddling sausage rolls and mince pies and urging people to help themselves to what remained of the cheese and French bread. Florence noticed that the satyr was impressed by her and that she seemed genuinely amused by him, replying quite saucily to his sallies. She had the trick of being on terms with a variety of people, an attribute of which Florence had not previously been aware.

'Egg nog,' Florence said, advancing on the Prentices, who had nudged their way into the sitting-room. They demurred, but she thrust glasses at them so firmly they had no choice but to accept. In the far corner of the room, edged between the pearl grey man and a pearl grey woman who must surely be his wife, Florence saw a man who was definitely a whisky candidate. She could not imagine how she had come to overlook him—perhaps he had arrived while she was disrobing the tiresome Prentices. Tall and broad-shouldered, he had the erect bearing of a man who has looked after himself well. A good head, Florence noted, and the confidence to let it be—what hair he had was close cropped. Florence liked a good head on a man. She liked, too, slightly slanting èyes, the flesh crinkled with humour. He looked at her in amusement as she swept his companions to one side to introduce herself. He must have been finding things very dull and was no doubt glad to come across a lively woman.

'I am Florence Müller, Sophia's sister,' she said, thrusting out her hand and holding her bosom high.

He gave a little bow. 'Thomas Challoner.'

'Ah, our near neighbour,' she said, dismissing whatever claims his companions might have with fine disregard. 'You haven't a drink; we must remedy that. Come with me.'

He raised his eyebrows in apology to the pearl grey people, but suffered himself to be led away.

'I am sure you prefer your whisky unadulterated,' Florence said, flashing a smile over her shoulder.

'I do, indeed.'

'Into the kitchen, then.'

He seemed unperturbed by the chaos of the kitchen. Florence hoped this indicated some lack in Frances's housekeeping; she did not like men who were incapable of perturbation.

'A very mixed bunch here,' she said in the loud, jolly voice which had gained her attention in many a club bar.

'A truly catholic community,' he

94

murmured.

'Really? I hadn't realised,' she said, pouring whisky. 'Some of them look distinctly Protestant to me.'

He accepted the glass, smiling at some joke he was not proposing to share with her. They talked for a few moments about the weather. She noted a certain reserve in his manner and hoped he was not the sort of man who always stands back, observing others with amused toleration and never giving away anything of himself. Then she remembered that there had been tragedies in his life. Obviously it would not do to speak of the son—Florence could think of no gloss which could be applied to suicide; but some mention of the death of the wife would be quite permissible, particularly in view of her own situation.

'Sophia told me about your wife,' she said. Perhaps one should just establish knowledge of the demise; after this length of time sympathy was hardly called for from a new acquaintance. As he showed no inclination to develop the theme, she said, 'As you probably know, my husband is very ill.'

'Yes, I had heard. How is he today?'

'Asleep, I think.'

He looked more amused than ever, but a little startled, too, as if she had told a doubtful joke.

'I am very upset, of course,' she said,

experiencing an uncharacteristic need to defend herself. 'It is difficult to imagine a future with no one to care for.' Her heart gave a little lurch; this was the first time she had posited a future alone. 'I am a very active person. What shall I do?'

'If my own experience is anything to go by, there are always reasons for activity,' he said kindly. She had hoped this was going to lead to a personal exchange, but he went on to talk about fences to be repaired and all the work arising from being a Commoner.

'But what do you do with your spare time?'

'I paint.'

This was a gift which Florence accepted eagerly. 'How splendid. Flowers? Landscapes?'

'Landscapes, mostly.'

'Oh, I should so like to see them.' She clasped her hands to her breast. 'I love landscapes—places I recognise. I like to know where I am in a painting.'

'You would certainly know with mine,' he said wryly. 'But I'm afraid they are not very good. I do it to amuse myself.'

'And to give pleasure to others, surely?' She looked at him roguishly. She was not a believer in the subtle approach; subtlety, in her experience, was wasted on most men, who only wanted someone to show an interest in them. 'I know something about

96

paintings. After all, I have lived with them around me. My husband paints.'

'Really?' His eyes told her he knew exactly what she was about.

'Very odd paintings, nothing I feel comfortable with. A friend once said they were good.' Beneath his amused, sceptical gaze she felt a need to establish her position as a lover of art. 'He knew a man who owned a small gallery and I took one of Konrad's paintings to this man. Konrad would be hopeless about selling himself, let alone a painting. The gallery man spent some time looking at the painting. He was as puzzled by it as I was, I think. He said it was very strong and original.'

She felt that enough had been said about Konrad's painting, but Challoner seemed interested. 'What was the painting?'

'Well, that was the problem.' She screwed up her eyes, remembering the gallery, Konrad's picture propped up on a table, the man standing back, looking at it, walking around it, talking in what she had considered a rather showing-off way: 'Here, in the foreground, we have the figure seated in the chair by the electric stove, sewing, the light from a standard lamp spilling over the bent shoulder; the face is intent, perhaps the eyes are a little strained, but it is the task which holds the woman's attention. All that seems to matter to her is the next stitch. And outside in the street we see light flashing in the sky and rubble falling, people running past her window. The far window shows a scene where there is no light from the explosion—a dark street, the outline of a woman's body, the glint of a knife held in an upraised hand by an attacker masked in shadow.'

Florence, assembling her memories, managed to convey something of this to Thomas Challoner, who asked, 'And what did he think of it as a painting?'

'He said it was beautifully executed, but that it didn't hold together. Obviously, it was about violence, chaos ... Look, you can't really be interested in this.'

'But I am.'

'Oh, very well, then. He went on to talk about the instability of life and the fragility of our peace, that sort of thing. But he didn't find it particularly chilling, certainly not apocalyptic.'

'Did you find it chilling or apocalyptic?'

'Well, you don't like to think all this is going on in the head of someone you know; but the picture itself didn't chill me, though I did think it was rather disagreeable.' Florence was pleased that the conversation was turning more towards herself and her understanding of art. 'I thought the woman herself was rather dull for someone occupying centre stage. And as for the people running past the window, I couldn't believe that one of them wouldn't have banged on the door if something had been really wrong. My friend said they were people living in parallel worlds, but I think he was a bit bothered about the woman. He said he thought perhaps she should have been scaled down.'

'And the colour? His use of colour is particularly striking—at least, so I have heard.'

'You can't have heard anything about Konrad's paintings, he is quite unknown. You must be thinking of someone else.'

'Yes, of course. It was just that your description of the painting reminded me of someone, I can't think who.' He put his glass down. 'This is disgraceful of me. I'm keeping you from your guests.'

Florence, who was rattled by his comment about colour, allowed him to escape. A few minutes later Anita came in. 'Oh, shit, Mother! What are you doing lurking in here? The Prentices are emitting leaving noises and we need to make the most of it. Some of these people are taking root.'

'I have told you I don't want to hear that word used over Christmas. Do you think it's possible your father has ever exhibited without our knowing?'

'Exhibited what?'

'His paintings, of course.'

'I shouldn't think so.'

'But his paintings are colourful.'

'So? Which are the Prentices' coats, do you remember?'

'They'd better come and find them.'

'You're not concentrating on this, are you? They're only considering the possibility of leaving. I can't very well frog-march them out here.' She selected a few garments from the top of the pile. 'I'll try these on them. At least it may turn people's minds homewards.'

After a few moments Florence followed her. As she came into the hall there was a noticeable dying down of conversation among the crudities. Never one to let curiosity go unsatisfied, she went up the stairs and paused on the landing, where she was rewarded by hearing the satyr declare that ''er will make a fine widder wumman'.

Anita had made her point and the party was breaking up. The front door had been opened and cold air brushed Florence's cheek. She went to the small landing window and saw the Prentices stumble out, heads butted into the storm. Then Thomas Challoner appeared on the doorstep and beside him, the boy, Andrew, face upturned and shining in the light of a coloured lantern which Sophia had hung there. Challoner bent down to listen to the boy and then put an arm round his shoulders. They, too, went down the path, the boy darting here and there in excitement but always returning to the sheltering figure of the man.

In the hall, someone had had the idea that the party should conclude with a carol and voices took up the strains of 'Oh come all ye faithful'.

*   *   *

No one in the world could be less guilty of wanting to be a hero, Terence thought as he abandoned the car. So why had he allowed this to happen to him? He should have let Anita go on her own. It was unlikely that she would find anyone else while spending Christmas supervised by her mother. There were several people who would have taken pity on him; he could by now be sitting comfortably in Thelma Armitage's centrally heated flat in Balham, or he might even have accepted the invitation in Amanda's eyes. So little was he instructed in the landscape of heroism that he thought of a walk in a blizzard only in terms of catching a bad cold. The trees, massed as distinct from hedgerow, suggested that he had reached the forest, but, this apart, he had no idea where he was. The trees would provide some shelter from the wind and presumably there would be clearings with human habitations. Florence had talked about the forest dwellers she

101

remembered in her youth and Terence, town-bred and a country hater, imagined they would have been fruitful and multiplied since then. Succour would be available, if required.

After a struggle, his fingers as cold as the lock, he managed to open the boot and immediately cut his hand on an icicle. Snow had found its way inside and a thin layer of ice had formed in the linings of his boots. His scarf was thick as a board. The Burberry Anita had bought him last Christmas was very cold but had at least been folded so that the inside remained dry. As he did not know where he was it seemed unlikely that he would find his way back to the car today, so he decided to take his overnight bag with him. He was fastidious and the thought of using someone else's toothbrush—or having no toothbrush at all—was repellent.

He had been walking for some time, becoming increasingly alarmed, when he came to a sign. Staggering up to it, he wiped away the snow only to be greeted by the injunction: BEWARE OF DEER. By now he was very cold, exhausted and desperately hungry. After an hour reminiscent of those nightmares where striving limbs make no progress he found himself back at the car. He sat on the bonnet, panting and snivelling, before setting out again. The possibility occurred to him that he was going to die.

This thought gained hold as, some twenty minutes later, he found himself slowly, painfully, rising to a level with the branches of trees. Looking up, he saw that the snow had stopped and above was a pale blue sky towards which he was agonisingly making his way. The trees stood back on either side, like a guard of honour watching his progress. Then, suddenly, out of this blueness, a great chariot appeared and descended upon him. He was flying through the air to the accompaniment of a chorus of astonished angel voices and the last noise he heard, as consciousness deserted him, was a prolonged howl as of a celestial air raid warning.

'Two broken ribs and a broken leg,' the voice informed Sophia over the telephone.

'Your grand-children, Mrs. Carteret, were they ... ?'

'Oh, just a few cuts and bruises, and, of course, they were very upset at first, but he took the full brunt of the impact. It was quite amazing watching from the window; I couldn't think what had happened. The toboggan seemed to explode and everyone floated around it, including Benjamin, who did a double somersault and landed flat on his back with all four paws in the air—a terrible indignity for which he has not yet forgiven us ... Of course there is no question of his being moved ... My dear, it is the least we can do ... In rather a lot of discomfort,

I'm afraid, but the doctor has promised to look in again tomorrow with a further supply of painkillers ... No, no messages. I got the impression he doesn't quite know what he wants to say at present.'

* * *

Pale sunlight slanted through the trees, played delicately on the snow and traced a film of gold on the branches of the apple tree in the middle of the lawn. It was a pleasing effect but conveyed no promise of warmth. If anything, the sun's impotence served only as a chill reflection of the cold.

After the other party-goers had left, Frances remained to help with the washing up. Florence was not deceived by this gesture. Frances was wearing a chunky cream roll-necked sweater, none too clean, and black corduroys and Florence was convinced she had come in this unfestive attire with the set purpose of tempting Nicholas out of doors. Neither of them had put in an appearance while the party was in progress. The only reason the girl had installed herself at the sink was because she intended to stay to tea. Florence said, 'And how are you going to get home?' Florence looked people straight in the eye when she spoke—even if it were only a matter of querying a recipe she would bear down on them with the whole force of her personality.

Frances, resolute if uncomfortable beneath this scrutiny, said that she would walk.

'If you don't mind my saying so, I think that is rather inconsiderate.' Florence flung this opinion down like a gauntlet. 'You must know we couldn't possibly let you go on your own in this weather.'

'I go out on my own in all weathers when you aren't here,' Frances retorted with more spirit than courtesy. When Frances had arrived, Florence, observing that she was dark for an English girl, had comforted herself with the reflection that this was not the flashing Mediterranean darkness, but the darkness of one of those velvety little animals rarely glimpsed abroad. Now, she noted with alarm how the flush of rose in the cheeks livened the face. 'But if there's any problem,' Frances went on, still uppity, 'I'm sure Thomas would come over for me. He'll have to take Jasper for a walk, anyway.'

Florence inspected the stains on a mug with interest. Frances was surprised that her response should silence Florence and felt she must have contravened some social convention as well as that of outstaying one's welcome. Her inspection completed, Florence said jovially, 'In which case there would be a confrontation between Jasper and Tobias.'

'It wouldn't be much of a confrontation. Jasper's afraid of Tobias.'

The kitchen door opened and Sophia came in carrying a tray she had brought down from Konrad's room.

'But he hasn't eaten anything,' Florence protested. 'And I made that soup specially.'

'Never mind. He's sleeping now.'

'And Anita?' The rejection of her soup had upset Florence. Her energy was suddenly spent and she looked crumpled as any elderly woman at the end of a party. The hair which had gleamed brightly while it stayed in place was now forlorn as an abandoned bird's nest and the muscles at the sides of the jaw sagged like over-filled purses. 'Where is Anita?' she asked fretfully. 'She can't spend the whole of Christmas being inconsolable. We should count ourselves fortunate. If Terence was going to have an accident, it's better he had it somewhere other than here, all things considered.'

Sophia picked up a teacloth and a handful of cutlery. 'Why don't you have a rest, Florence. You've worked so hard. Frances and I will finish in here.'

Sophia and Frances worked in silence for some time after Florence departed. Sophia, who had allowed the party to take its course, seemed not so much tired as distanced. She laid the familiar objects on the kitchen table as if she had been away for a long time and was surprised to find them still in use. Every so often she stopped, staring down at the pattern of the oilcloth covering and once she stroked it gently, then fisted her fingers. The muscles of jaw and throat tensed with the effort to swallow.

Frances looked out of the window, watching the slanting shadows of the trees, the blue of evening encroaching on the sparkling sunlit lawn, hoping for the first sight of Nicholas, who had gone to see if he could dig at least one of the cars free. He appeared to be in no hurry. She said, fiercely wringing out the dishcloth, 'It's a load of old rubbish, all that business about lovers choosing one night of love as worth the price of eternal torment. It's not even worth the price of a flat battery.'

It seemed unsurprising that she should say this in front of Sophia, since it was Sophia's presence which had wrenched the words from her, just as Sophia had so often led people on by saying, 'You think ... ?' 'You don't perhaps ... ?' and then the other person would pick up that floating sentence and complete it for her. This time she had done it without being aware of any involvement, and she had to drag her attention to Frances as if there were a heavy weight on her eyes.

'You put that into my mind,' Frances said.

Sophia did not confront the girl as

Florence had done. She studied her sideways from beneath lowered lids, a wry, tentative smile hovering about her lips as if waiting permission to share a discovery which she wondered if Frances might be able to accept. Her appraisal of the girl was tactful. She said, 'I seem to remember that in *Hassan* it was the woman who made the choice.'

'You think love never comes first with a man?'

'Do you think it should? Would you want Nicholas so much if you thought he would be with you always, that nothing else called him?'

Frances looked with aching intensity at the golden light on the apple tree. 'I want one perfect moment.'

'A lifetime of imperfect moments wouldn't sustain you?'

'I expect it would sustain me a whole lot better. Is that what you're telling me?'

'I have nothing to tell you, Frances. It's just that I'm not sure what you mean by perfect.'

'I call that perfect,' pointing beyond the window. 'Now, this minute, while the glow lasts.'

But already the golden light was withdrawing and the apple tree was no longer transformed. And Nicholas, was he, then, only the bearer of this much-desired thing, not himself the glory? 'I don't mind how it is,' she said stubbornly. 'I only know I want it. He can go away afterwards. I know he will go away next week, and I shan't make a misery for him or myself. I shan't blame.'

Sophia, looking at her face, thought that there was much of the child in Frances still—a child dazzled by the tinsel and the gold and silver balls, a child crying for the fairy on the Christmas tree.

'Let's warm up some of that punch,' said Sophia, who was not above such remedies for sickness of heart. 'It's supposed to be for tomorrow, but we have plenty.'

'I'm very selfish,' Frances said as she was sipping the punch; this was more an acknowledgement than a cause for contrition. 'I haven't asked about Konrad. I knew I couldn't in front of Florence and then I forgot.'

Sophia said, 'Never mind,' and Frances accepted this as an absolution and forgot about Konrad again.

Out in the garden, Nicholas had finished work on his car. The light was failing. He put the shovel back in the boot and walked slowly down the garden path, pausing for a moment to look at the snow, deep blue in between the trees. Frances saw him standing there, hands in pockets, like a man on a street corner, trying to solve the great problem of nowhere to go.

*   *   *

It was early evening. The cottage was quiet. Florence was aware of the stillness as soon as she woke, indeed it seemed to have woken her, this absence of meaningful activity. She lay for a time listening to the creaks and groans as the cold tightened its grip on the bones of the cottage. Soon, she heard Nicholas return from taking Frances home and she said angrily, 'She means to have him.' There seemed nothing she could do about it which would not antagonise Thomas Challoner. This was one of the most interesting men she had met in a long time and his presence was the only thing that would make Christmas Day bearable. She would have to suffer Frances. Of course, the girl was not attractive—she lacked charm and seemed to see no need for it—but Florence sensed that she was very strong. She was the sort of person who brought about the things she wanted. Nicholas was hopelessly weak, but his very weakness had helped him to escape before. Now, Florence was aware of some weakening of his resolve to escape. She was not particularly perceptive where other people were concerned provided their interests did not conflict with her own; but she was very quick to pick up any signals that meant danger to herself. The hairs on the back of her neck had risen at her first sight of Terence. Now she sensed desperation in Nicholas as an animal senses fear.

Florence sat up on one elbow. Her lamp was burning low and the symbolism was not lost on her. She felt a need to cry, something she had rarely experienced since childhood. Why was nothing happening? Why had no one switched on the radio—there must be a carol service on one of the wavelengths, surely? Sophia had a transistor, but perhaps the battery was not working. If that was the case, Nicholas must get into town and buy one; they couldn't go through Christmas with no television and no radio. And what was Anita doing? And why was Konrad sleeping so much? It must be the painkillers. Sophia must telephone the doctor and ask if they could cut down on them. She pulled on her dressing gown and opened the door cautiously in case Tobias was outside, awaiting the opportunity to get into a warm bed. Faintly, she could hear voices in the kitchen. She went down the stairs—narrowly missing her daughter as Anita went into Konrad's room—adding up in her mind the things Nicholas could do while he was in town.

*　　*　　*

On the mantelshelf in Konrad's room there

was a wooden carving of a boy playing a fiddle to a bear. Anita had not noticed it standing there on the previous occasion when she had come into the room. Now she went to the mantelshelf and stared at the carving. Both the boy and the bear danced: the boy, one leg crooked sideways, was ugly and graceless; the bear, forepaws spread at shoulder level, one pointed toe crossing the other, was nimble as a Scottish dancer. Although it was beautifully carved, there was a zestful crudeness in the figures, particularly that of the boy. Anita remembered the little piece well; as a child it had fascinated her because it was at once droll and macabre.

Where had it come from? She was sure it had not been made in England. It was old; once it had been painted, but now only a few flakes of green and red and brown remained. Had it belonged to Konrad's father, his mother? She moved to the bed, as though he might yet provide the answer. 'The dancing boy,' she said softly. 'Whose was it originally? Where did it come from?' She felt her own history was tied up in the little carving. As a child she had not been curious about her parents' background—perhaps because her mother had talked so much about her own childhood and how undervalued she had been because 'I am one of the Marthas of the world ...' All her memories of her father were centred in

112

herself: her father teaching her to ride a bicycle, fetching her from parties, telling her stories, dressing up as Father Christmas at her own children's party. As a psychologist, she knew that children's pictures of their parents tend to be self-centred, concerned with their own care, protection, amusement; children imagine that their parents have no life other than that in which they themselves figure. She knew also that this illusion tends to persist in the face of the evidence as children become adults. The last remnant of childhood is in the parent. Even her own emancipated generation was no exception, using their parents as a back-stop and imagining them relatively ageless, as able at seventy to fetch and carry, care and provide as they had been in their prime.

All this Anita knew. But where her father was concerned her powers of analysis deserted her. Just as she herself had never truly escaped from her mother, so she in her turn had never let her father go. When she had grown away from him, it was as though he had ceased to function once her back was turned. Perhaps the fact that he had no roots in England, no demonstrable past in the form of parents, brothers, sisters, that no letters came bearing foreign stamps, that there were no photographs to which he could point and say, 'This is where I lived as a child,' perhaps all this had contributed to her attitude. Yet, even allowing for that, her lack of curiosity now struck her as unnatural. She had never been interested in her foreign grandparents, had never asked about the place where he was born, and he had never talked about that distant childhood, perhaps had not been able to. She did not know how bad his memories were. Although he was a Catholic, there was Jewish blood in the family and none of his relatives had survived the war. But he had told her stories with a Russian background, several of them about circus life. As she listened to those strange tales, which must have been told to him by his mother or even one of his grandmothers, was she learning something of the family history? Or had he himself, possibly because he could do it no other way, recreated the past in those stories?

'I need to know,' she said. 'The stories you told me when I was a child, did you make them up or were they handed down to you?'

He lay still, his breathing a little laboured, but not painfully so, each breath expelled with the sort of noise Tobias made when he was trying to get rid of a fur ball in his throat.

She took his hand. 'I need to know because I love you,' she said. His fingers pressed her hand. It was the kind of thing a person might do when they were listening to music intently, yet wished to reassure a demanding, anxious companion.

114

She sat quietly, holding his hand, and as she did so a thought occurred to her. Wherever it was he came from all those years ago, he had brought one thing with him. She got up and returned to look at the carved figure, her interest kindled sharply. She was holding it in her hands when Sophia came into the room. Their eyes met and Sophia looked straight this time, no sidelong glance.

'He has been here before,' Anita said.

'Yes.'

'All those painting weekends?'

'Yes.'

'I don't know how I feel about this.' Anita seemed to address the remark to the boy with the fiddle, rather than Sophia. 'My mother didn't deceive him, you know; she's just rather greedy. She could never leave one chocolate in the box.'

'Did your mother ever ask him for particulars of where he went on those weekends?'

'So long as he didn't turn our attic spare room into a studio, I don't think it bothered her where he painted. But she did believe he went away to paint.'

'We can't talk about this now. Later we may have to, but not now.'

She was quite without shame. Anita, who thought that older people unnecessarily complicated sex with feelings of guilt and the need to justify, was considerably put out by the lack of any such need in her aunt. She went out of the room, imagining her cup of woe to be filled to the brim, only to become aware as she went down the stairs of a terrible moaning coming from the kitchen. Here she found Nicholas and Florence. Florence was weeping over the table, rocking to and fro, while Nicholas stood by looking as if he were facing a firing squad, gazing towards an eternity concealed behind the doors of the dresser.

Anita said, 'What is this all about?'

Florence turned on her as if in the middle of a fierce argument. 'Of course I knew; you didn't think I didn't know he was going to die? But not now.' She turned away, cradling her breasts and rocking again. 'Next week, perhaps, but not now.'

Anita looked at Nicholas.

He said wearily, 'When we arrived and Sophia saw him, she sent for a priest. She said the blizzard would get worse and he mightn't outlive it.'

'So he has received the last rites?' A person who was not Anita but whom she carried around with her and on whom she relied to create the right impression—on this occasion, calmness—addressed Nicholas. 'Why didn't you tell us?'

'There's hardly been an opportunity, has there? I thought it better to wait until we had a few quiet moments together, the three of us.'

'When have we ever had one quiet moment together, let alone a few?'

'How can you speak like that?' Florence rose unsteadily from the table, slapping away the hand Nicholas stretched out to help her. 'I have always had time for you; whenever you needed me I was there, ready with advice and comfort.'

'But not to listen,' Nicholas said coldly. For a moment, the vagueness that blurred his features cleared as if a mist had lifted revealing a wintry prospect, its outlines pared to the bone, sharp and stark as it was unforgiving.

Florence put a hand to her breast, a gesture not entirely histrionic. She closed her eyes and made an effort to stem the weeping; sounds came from her windpipe like a person who has swallowed a pea the wrong way snatching for breath. Anita went to the sink and filled a glass with water. Florence drank, slopping the water down her chin and on to the front of her blouse. She thrust the empty glass at Anita and turned to Nicholas.

'You're upset by this. I understand.' She patted his arm. 'But you must pull yourself together. I'm going to need you.'

He backed away. Anita said, 'Don't be such a shit, Nicholas.' Florence rounded on Anita. 'I have asked you not to use that word. Have you no consideration for me, not

117

even at this time?' While Florence's attention was distracted from him, Nicholas left the room.

Florence collapsed on to the kitchen chair, which rocked uneasily beneath the weight of her distress. 'What is happening?' she moaned. 'What can be happening to me?'

'You'd better go and lie down,' Anita said.

'You want to get rid of me. You want to push me out of the way.'

As this was exactly what Anita did want, she felt she could not persist. 'Come in to the sitting-room, then. It will be more comfortable there.'

In the sitting-room, to Anita's surprise, Florence sat quietly, staring first at one object and then another as if seeking a clue to her whereabouts. From time to time she shivered. When Anita went to pull the curtains, she said sharply, 'No, leave them. This room is small enough as it is.' Anita busied herself adjusting the oil lamp. The wick was burning low. 'Darkness is all we need,' she thought.

Florence said, 'How can Sophia live here alone?' The question was not rhetorical. 'What does she do when we're not here?' This was her first essay in imagining other people existing when she was not present and she soon abandoned it. 'It's not natural. Not a natural way of life. I have always been a very natural woman.' She went on talking, half to herself, plucking at the pleats of her kilt.

The front door opened and closed. They could hear footsteps crunching the frozen snow. Anita went to the window and saw Nicholas striding across the garden in the direction of the path which led eventually to the Challoners' house. She dreaded her mother's question, but when she turned away from the window she saw that Florence was asleep.

Anita went into the kitchen and prepared ham sandwiches. She made coffee, put mince pies to heat and peeled a banana. She sat at the kitchen table and ate slowly and steadily, staring at the flickering candle flame for so long that when she turned away a dark negative of the flame seemed to be implanted in her eyes. She put sandwiches on a plate, poured a cup of milk and took the tray into the sitting-room. Florence was still asleep, so she scribbled a note on the back of a Christmas card—mince pies in oven. Then, at last, she went up the stairs to Konrad's room.

Sophia was sitting by the bed, holding Konrad's hand. Anita wanted to tell her how wicked she was, but did not know how much her father could hear, or how near the end was. She wouldn't want these to be the last words he heard. Instead, she whispered, 'Will it be tonight?' Sophia shook her head.

It did not occur to Anita to challenge Sophia's judgement. 'I'll take a turn,' she said and Sophia nodded.

Anita sat with her father, holding his hand, while Sophia went down to the kitchen and ate the mince pies that Anita had left for Florence. Then she went out to the shed where she was sleeping and where Tobias was waiting for her. It was an hour before she returned.

'I'm all right,' Anita said, although in fact she felt rather faint because her father's rasping breath occasioned an answering pain in her own breast.

'Your mother isn't all right,' Sophia said. 'You must look after her. She is very shocked.'

Anita was taken aback to realise that she felt more at one with Sophia, for all her wickedness, than with her mother. She went reluctantly down the stairs and, after a brief search, found Florence in the scullery among the boots.

'There must be some that will fit me,' Florence said. 'I have normal-sized feet.'

'It matters?' Anita tried not to sound weary of her mother's antics.

'Of course it matters. I can't walk barefoot—though I dare say it would be fitting.' Florence seemed to have recovered some of her sharpness.

'What are you talking about? Where do

you think you can walk tonight, barefoot or otherwise?'

'To Mass, of course, what else?'

'You must be mad. The church is miles away.'

'Two miles, according to Sophia. If we start now we should make it.'

Anita realised that this must be taken seriously. Her mother did not make empty gestures of this nature; if she said she meant to do something or go somewhere, it was usually within her capacity to achieve her end. Anita could remember returning one Christmas Eve very tired after Mass and her mother announcing that what she fancied was a Baked Alaska. She had set about making it there and then. But at least the ingredients had been to hand. Ingredients of another kind would be involved in this lunatic journey and they were definitely not to hand.

'You haven't the stamina,' she told Florence. 'And even if you had, you've no sense of direction at the best of times, which this isn't. The only car that is free of the snow is Nicholas's and he has the keys. Added to which, if we didn't die on our way to the road, we would almost certainly find it impassable when we got there.'

Florence said, pulling on a boot, 'How would it have been if the Three Wise Men had turned back so readily?'

'They came late, if you recall.'

'You needn't come if you don't want to. But I have to go.'

'Lots of people are going to miss Mass tonight.'

'I have to go.'

There was no doubting the urgency of this assertion. Anita saw that whatever she said, her mother meant to set out. She went upstairs and explained to Sophia. 'How can I stop her?'

'Better to let her go. Something is driving her out there.'

'But it doesn't make sense.'

'Oh, sense—it's late in the day for sense.' 'Oh well, I suppose no harm will come of it. We shan't get very far. She's not a walker. When she goes up Richmond Hill she runs out of puff.'

'Nicholas has gone for a drink with Thomas. I expect he'll be back soon. I'll send him after you. And you'd better take the first-aid box from the bathroom, just in case, and a little brandy.' Sophia came down to the front door to watch them set out. 'Be careful to keep to the path. It hasn't snowed since our guests left and you should be able to follow in their tracks.' Most of those tracks will at some point go off to forest dwellings, Anita thought, but as she did not expect to go far before her mother lost heart, she did not protest.

It seemed unnatural, for all her talk of being a natural woman, that Florence should have this urge to get out to Mass at a time when her husband was about to die. Anita said, 'Don't you want to see him before we go? You haven't been to him since you took up that soup after the party.'

'No, no. I have to get to Mass. Can't you understand?' Florence was eager to set out. It seemed to Anita that her mother thought Konrad's life would be extended if she could fulfil this commitment, that even in the matter of his dying she could bring her influence to bear.

The wind had dropped now. It was still as they stood on the threshold; the air fitted their faces close as a film of ice. Anita said, 'You're sure about this?' Florence, who had been looking up as if mesmerised by the glitter of stars, launched herself forward and immediately disappeared in drifted snow which had piled up around the walls of the cottage. The fact that Anita and Sophia were able to rescue her without undue difficulty boosted her confidence and she set off down the garden path with determination.

In much less time than Anita would have thought possible the cottage disappeared into the snow as if it had never been. Tracks there were—holes around which the snow foamed—whether made by animals or humans it was hard to tell. The path was strewn with obstacles; branches of trees—indeed whole trees—had fallen during the hurricane of 1987 and the gales that had followed and lay propped against other trees, forming great walls of snow over which Anita and Florence must climb. 'We couldn't have got the car along here yesterday,' Anita said. 'We must have taken a wrong track.' But they went on because it seemed less hazardous than turning back and perhaps taking yet another wrong track. Already they were not thinking very clearly. At each step their boots sank deep in snow and an effort was required to raise them again. After what seemed an unconscionable time, they came to what was obviously a ride between the trees and Florence was convinced they were on course again. Anita maintained the ride was broader than any track they had followed in the car.

'I remember it quite well,' Florence insisted. 'And, anyway, we couldn't possibly have missed a track as broad as this when we came.' This, it seemed to Anita, was to be not so much a trial of stamina as of optimism.

Although the snow came up to the top of her boots, Florence stumbled forward eagerly as if in the far distance the church were already in sight. From time to time, she encouraged Anita: 'We shall see them soon. There will be so many people, all going ...

we shall see them.' They had now been out for over three-quarters of an hour. Still Florence struggled on, seeing the people and the church doors open, the light from inside casting a golden glow on the snow, hearing the sound of music and the laughter of excited children. Her expectancy increased with every foot of ground so heroically gained. She had always been expectant, had never allowed herself to dwindle into a state of dulled acceptance; but this was something the like of which she had never experienced before. Expectancy throbbed in her temples, pressed against her ribcage ... Suddenly, she missed her footing and sprawled across the dismembered trunk of a tree. The breath was knocked out of her and with it went the throng of people, the church, the golden light. All faded. Her child, now grown into a cross, disparaging adult, was squatting behind a tree to relieve herself. There was a brand across Florence's forehead and a searing pain in her lungs. She was no longer sure if it was she or Konrad who was about to die. Death, not birth, seemed in the air this night.

Anita came and propped her mother up against the tree stump. 'Now's the time for a little brandy,' she said. They had a swig each and then sat silently, hunched like spent athletes who have failed to touch the tape. Florence said, 'To be born on a night like this! It's not at all the way I have thought of it.' She sounded just as she used to when criticising the way a director was producing a crucial scene in a play at her amateur dramatic club. She turned to Anita. 'Why do you think He chose to come in winter? It's very hard to understand what good could possibly come out of such cold.'

Anita put her arm round her mother's shoulders, gingerly, as if she feared she might never get it back again. 'Are we going on?'

'I can't,' Florence said simply. 'I can't go a step further. I don't know why I came. It seemed important at the time, but I can't remember why.'

When Sophia told her that Konrad had received the last rites, Death had become a reality in whose presence she herself had seemed to fall apart, reduced to the level of the homely clutter in the kitchen. All the characteristics and qualities so necessary to her self-assurance had been swept away, like friends who have failed in the hour of need. Threatened by disintegration, she had rushed out in great fear, not seeking absolution so much as hoping that the tattered pieces which had made her what she was might be picked up on her journey and brought to a place where they would be reassembled in some recognisable form.

'If we're not going on, we must go back,' Anita said.

'I haven't the strength.' Florence began to cry, not passionately, but wearily, like an overtaxed child.

'We can't stay still,' Anita said. 'Whatever else we do, we mustn't stay still.'

'Everything is still,' Florence said. 'Hadn't you noticed?'

Where were they all, the forest creatures? Florence imagined the birds frozen on branches, deer stopped in mid-stride; foxes lying on their backs with folded front paws. No breath in any of them. All her life Florence had made it her business to fill every gap in conversation and she had come to believe that only the sound of the human voice sustained the universe. But the silence had always been there, in the background, waiting like a tireless enemy; now it seemed it had won.

'It is all over,' she said to Anita. 'I, too, shall lie down and fold my front paws.'

Anita, frightened, tried to haul her mother to her feet, but Florence was a heavy woman and her clothing had added to her weight. Anita hooked her arms under her mother's armpits and clasped her hands across the substantial chest. She began to drag Florence along the path, while Florence stared up at the stars winking in the black sky. They did not get very far before Anita backed into a fallen branch and fell heavily. When she had recovered her breath, Anita began to shout at her mother. 'We shall die here if we don't move, do you realise that? You may be ready to die, but I'm not.' She struck her mother across the face, something she had wanted to do ever since she was a child, but not in these circumstances. She took hold of the front of her mother's sheepskin jacket and attempted to shake her. Florence seemed beyond caring and all Anita succeeded in doing was to frighten herself still more.

Florence, who was now feeling light-headed and rather exalted, said, 'I don't care. I don't mind what happens. You had better—' She stopped abruptly, sat up straight and pointed a finger.

'No hallucinations, please!' Anita said, but she turned her head and saw two lights gleaming under one of the trees. Not a fox, she thought, too high for that. She made her way forward, heart pounding, and came upon a short, stumpy pony. He made no movement when she reached out to touch his mane, but his eyes blinked.

'He's frozen,' she shouted to her mother. 'He's nearly frozen to death, poor thing.' She took off her scarf and set to work frantically rubbing the pony's mane and flanks. Florence struggled to her feet and stumbled towards her daughter. Together, they occupied themselves with the pony for some time. 'What are we going to do with him?'

Florence asked when at last he showed signs of thawing.

'You are going to sit on him.'

This was easier said than done. What the pony lacked in height it made up for in girth and Florence was no horsewoman.

'You're supposed to grip with your knees,' Anita said in exasperation.

'There's nothing to grip and, anyway, I have no knees. Both my legs are frostbitten, I shall probably lose them.' Eventually, however, she managed to squat froglike, gripping the pony's mane.

The pony had submitted amiably to these proceedings, but none of Anita's blandishments, no shouting, poking, prodding, or pulling on his mane, could move him.

'He expects to be led,' Florence said indifferently, looking down on the scene as if from a great height.

'I'm trying to lead him.'

'Not in the way to which he is accustomed.' Florence's lofty position had elevated her to the role of instructor. 'You need something with which to pull him along.'

The pony rubbed its muzzle against Anita's shoulder. 'You see,' Florence said. 'He's quite friendly, but stupid. You need a rope.'

Anita tried to make a rope of her scarf, but

the pony's neck was remarkably thick and the scarf acted as a muffler rather than a rope. Then she thought of the first-aid box. She unzipped her backpack and extracted the small case that Sophia had given her. As she had hoped, it contained a roll of bandage; but there was not enough to form an adequate rope. She stood thinking, chewing a strand of hair as she had as a child when trying to solve a mathematical problem. It had always seemed that her hair had magical properties. 'I've got the answer!' she exclaimed. The first-aid box contained as well as the bandage, a pair of scissors and a roll of adhesive tape. She took a swathe of hair and began to plait. It was her proud boast that she could sit on her hair, so the plait was long. When she had made four plaits, she took the scissors and cut them loose high in the nape of the neck; then she joined them into one long rope with the adhesive tape.

'You will look very ugly,' Florence said. 'And I expect at one tug it will all come apart.'

'The hair is strong and so is the tape, and we'll have to hope he doesn't tug.'

She fitted the rope around the pony's neck and gently urged him forward. He followed meekly, his scruples apparently satisfied.

Nicholas, setting out to meet them, had one of the most unnerving experiences in all his explorations, when he saw coming along the path towards him what appeared to be a huddled figure on a donkey led by a man.

*   *   *

It was after eleven by the time Florence had been settled in bed. While Sophia was tending her, the telephone rang.

'Whoever was that on the phone?' she asked Nicholas when eventually she came downstairs.

'A Mrs. Prentice, I think she said. Her voice was very faint.'

'Something left behind? The Prentices usually leave a memento of their visits.'

'I think it's more a case of their having taken something away with them. She asked if we were all right. It seems they're not.'

CHAPTER THREE

At dawn a smoky sun had cast a crimson glow on the snow on the window sill of Konrad's room; but now the colour had gone from the sky and it was colder. He thought he could hear the ice ringing like the notes of a piano. Stillness, cessation of breath, the earth hung suspended, without motion. But the earth couldn't do that, of course, not until its appointed time. It was he who was suspended.

It seemed natural, this stepping out of time with all its weariness, no more than shedding an old garment.

Distance. Everything distanced. Distance from pain, fear, anger, pathetic attempts at loving and caring; distance from people. At first it had been no more than a hairline crack in reality, something that could be righted by a little attention, increased concentration; but it had grown until it was a chasm which there was no bridging. The distance would not now be lessened.

There they were, the people in the cottage, like figures in a child's toy theatre, coming and going, resentful, awkward, upset, apprehensive, and one who was silent and loving. He was somewhere outside, looking in at them. They had no reality. God was the only reality; no longer the object of pious devotion, but the one incontrovertible truth beside which all else was shadow.

He would like to have been benevolent, he felt an impulse to benevolence of a general kind; but the intricacies of relationship, the needs and demands, excuses and accusations, responsibilities, the remembrance of things said and done, of particular acts of love or hate, had no meaning any more. He had passed into an area where they had no currency.

'It is like being in a hammock,' he said, suddenly, clearly, to Sophia. 'Still held by gravity, but not earthed.'

When she came to his side he had drifted away. Suppose he slips away finally while I am not with him? she thought. How hard to accept that there is this great occasion in the lives of those we love in which we play no part.

She wondered what it would feel like for him, and for herself when her time came. Tiredness at the end of a day when nothing is of more importance than sleep and the faces of even the most dearly loved grow dim and finally dissolve?

I must let you go, she thought; whatever form we take hereafter I shall never find you again unless I let this mortal man go. Our only hope is in the letting go.

*   *   *

Anita woke painfully aware of every bone in her body. When she tried to look at the clock on the chest of drawers beside the bed, she found that her head was locked in the forward position. She forced herself to sit up, just to make sure she could still do it. It was eight o'clock and dull light filtered through the curtains. She managed to get out of bed and stand up after the third attempt. Drawing the curtains proved difficult

133

because it was excruciatingly painful to raise her arm to shoulder level. Nicholas was standing just below the window feeding a small, stout pony. What she had hoped was a terrible dream became concrete.

She turned stiffly, like a soldier, and faced the mirror. The great twisted tangle, which greeted her every morning and which shielded her from the cool inspection of first light, was gone. What had always been a subsidiary something in the centre round which the abundant hair cascaded now stood out boldly, each feature clarified as though an equation had been resolved overnight. She saw eyes set too close so that they seemed to be crowding the long, patrician nose which appeared understandably not to approve of the full mouth and heavy jaw. It was as though she had spent years sculpting blindfold and now was presented with a head quite unlike the work of her imagination. The face expressed clearly its dissatisfaction with what had happened to it. It was also tremendously sad, as though it had had a right to expect something better.

There was a knock on the door and Sophia came into the room. 'Are you all right?' she asked in a tone which permitted a negative response.

'You have eyes,' Anita said miserably.

'I've brought my scissors—perhaps I can tidy it up a bit. At least you're lucky that it's so curly.'

'It's not the hair that worries me; it's the face.'

'You'll get used to it.'

'And the neck. Look at the length of that neck. I look like Alice after she drank the potion. My head's just a little blip on the end of a stalk.'

'You can wear a scarf until you get used to it.'

'And it's very stiff, my neck. It's not accustomed to the feel of air and last night was no time to start exposing it.'

Sophia picked up the eiderdown and wrapped it round Anita's shoulders. 'It's cold in here. Let's go into the bathroom. Nicholas is out and Florence is still asleep.'

'Were you with my father all night?' Anita asked as they passed Konrad's room on the way to the bathroom. 'How is he?'

'The same. Nicholas sat with him half the night.'

'I'd like to be with him this morning.'

Sophia succeeded in giving some shape to the shorn head, but Anita complained, 'I look like someone who's come badly out of a major operation.'

'What is it that you don't like? Is it what you see—or is it the image which will be presented to other people that troubles you?'

'I'm not sure.' Anita was looking in the mirror, turning her head from side to side,

135

her eyes screwed up as if she dared not confront the image. 'It frightens me—like a doppelgänger.'

★　　★　　★

Florence rose like a cork on water, physically none the worse for her experience of the night before. She was convinced, so rested did she feel, that in some miraculous way she had surmounted her troubles—more than surmounted, had conquered them. She had gone out into the wood like a knight errant to pit her strength against a dragon, and she had slain it. In this triumphant frame of mind she pulled on her dressing gown and went to the bathroom, pausing at the top of the stairs to call 'Happy Christmas' to Sophia and Anita whom she could hear talking below. When she had washed she went into Konrad's room. 'It is Christmas morning, my darling,' she said. He did not open his eyes, but it seemed to her that his breathing was easier, if rather shallow.

She sat beside him and took his hand in hers. 'We must pray together. You can recover. All things are possible.' But even as she said this she became less sure—as though by speaking the words she had fallen into one of those traps so randomly distributed in the path of people who seek to slay dragons. She was visited by the notion that had come to

136

her when she first arrived here, that she had entered a world where the commonsense everyday rules no longer applied. A world of no-sense. A world, in fact, horribly like that depicted in Konrad's paintings.

She tried to compose herself for prayer. In spite of many disappointments, she had always been on good terms with God, able to talk to him sharply in her youth about the way his Son had preferred Mary to Martha—'I'm the kind who will raise a family and keep a home going, without my kind there wouldn't be a Mary to sit at His feet'; and as an adult, to explain seeming waywardness—'I have to give; it's all a matter of giving. If I get pleasure out of it, that surely doesn't make it wrong?' But now, just when she had been feeling so exalted, the flow of communication abruptly dried up. Either He was no longer listening or there was something she could not put into words. It was unusual for her to recognise such a lack in her ability to articulate; but as she sat looking at Konrad she became aware of something wrong that could not be diagnosed, like an indigestible substance heavy in her stomach that obstinately refused to be sicked up. She decided to sing instead of praying. Perhaps it was the view from the window that made her choose 'In the bleak midwinter'. She returned to her room feeling chastened.

As she dressed, memories of other Christmases came unbidden to her mind. Arrival here, at her grandmother's cottage, her eyes eagerly seeking the crib in the hall. She had wanted all the figures in at once—the whole gorgeous impact of it—and had never understood why the Wise Men had to wait until a time when her enthusiasm had waned before they made an appearance. As she grew older she had come to like the word Epiphany but had not been reconciled to the waiting.

Her grandmother had not approved of Christmas trees and so there had never been one, only a candle at the window; but the forest trees had made good this lack. How friendly the great firs had seemed then, planted there for her delight.

Ever since they were very small, until the death of her grandmother when Florence was eleven, the children had performed a Nativity play. This had included the proclamation to Mary because Florence always insisted on being the Virgin and a decent part had to be found for Sophia. So Sophia as the Angel of the Annunciation had rather more in the way of tinsel and spangles about her costume than Florence was allowed. As the years passed Florence had come to wonder if she had made the right choice. Her cousin Martin had played Joseph and the shepherds and each of the Wise

Men. When Florence had protested that this was unfair her mother had pointed out that she could not relinquish her care of the baby in order to play other parts. Her grandmother had said, 'Martin is a boy,' which meant that it was appropriate for him not only to play the male roles, but to hog the stage as well. Sophia had hovered unconcerned above this controversy, representing the angel host in a satin bedspread. Florence resolved that when she herself had a baby she would not let it prevent her playing as many roles as she chose.

She remembered, as she put the finishing touches to her hair, how, after they had taken down their stockings and had rushed into their parents' and grandmother's bedrooms to display their treasures and then been told they were to keep quiet while the grown-ups performed all the tedious tasks essential to their toilet, she had tiptoed down the stairs.

The little hall and the rooms leading off it had had the hushed expectancy of spaces on a stage, awaiting the appearance of the actors. At any moment, the door would open and a story would unfold. The sitting-room was the centre, the source of the magic. It was so tidy that Florence was overawed, as she was on the rare occasions when she saw her mother and father in evening dress.

Every vase and carefully placed ornament seemed to glisten like jewels. Someone had come down very early and lit the fire: the flames flickered and the logs crackled to an unseen audience. On the side tables and on the window-ledge were boxes of dates and peppermint creams, bowls of walnuts and brazil nuts, round wooden boxes of Turkish Delight. Christmas roses formed a garland for a small portrait of the Virgin and Child. A heap of fir cones sprinkled with jack frost supported the candles in the centre of the window. All these things anticipated a great event which never quite happened, though each year, beyond the time when she was too old for such fantasies, Florence hoped for the knock on the door and the strange woman standing there seeking shelter for herself and her baby, which, her grandmother assured her, had been known to happen in the forest.

Once she had told her priest about this and he had said, 'That kind of Christmas is for children', and she had pointed out to him that Jesus had said 'Except ye be converted, and become as little children, ye shall not enter into the kingdom of heaven.' He had had nothing to say to that. She had not been lucky with priests. In the films of her youth a character stumbled into a church in need and there was this homely priest with a smile-wrinkled face played by Spencer Tracy and in no time their problem had been resolved. Or it was Henry Fonda and the script was by Graham Greene and he was a failed priest with nothing to offer except his own agony. In her times of need all Florence seemed to get was Henry Fonda without the shared agony. People didn't listen to her, that was the trouble; although one exasperated man had had the temerity to say that she didn't listen to him but came equipped with her own solutions. Oh dear, what had come over her? Here she was, arguing with herself on Christmas morning when any moment she must go down to breakfast during which Anita would provide argument in plenty.

Anita provided not only an argument but a shock. Florence had always maintained that putting up one's hair was a sign of maturity. Cutting it off was another matter altogether. 'What possessed you to do that to yourself, I can't imagine,' she said.

'You said we had to have a rope.'

'I have no recollection of saying anything of the sort. Your face is too long for that style. You don't look like my daughter.'

'Not bad,' Anita said. 'Two out of three. You forgot to mention how hideous Ingrid Bergman looked in *For Whom the Bell Tolls*.'

They were interrupted by the ringing of the telephone. 'My turn,' Anita said.

'I seem to have heard the phone several times this morning,' Florence said to Sophia.

'A number of people have been taken ill with some form of food poisoning.'

'What do they expect from us?'

'Penitence, I think.'

'How absurd.'

Anita came back. 'Mrs. Prentice with a further bulletin. In a period of recollection during the night it came to her that none of us drank the egg nog.'

'How very stupid. The woman obviously has a weak stomach. I recall thinking what an unhealthy colour her face was when she arrived. But, of course, we must visit.'

'You may visit. I'm going to see Terence.'

'I suppose these people's doctors have been informed?'

'I think it's safe to say that few of the doctors in the neighbourhood are enjoying a quiet Christmas with their families,' Sophia answered.

Anita began to collect the crockery. 'The only reason we haven't had a visitation is that telephone communication with the health inspectorate appears to have broken down.' As she went out of the door, she said, 'And how you can go out visiting when Father is dying, I can't imagine.'

'One's children can be so cruel,' Florence said to Sophia. Then, seeing that Sophia was about to follow Anita, 'Don't go rushing away like that. We haven't had a moment together since I arrived.' Sophia sat down again, but offered no conversation.

'I can't stay with Konrad for long,' Florence said, as though answering unspoken criticism. 'I just can't, Sophia. He lies there without apparently being aware of my presence, yet he doesn't seem to be doing his dying at all passively. Instead of my comforting him, as soon as I am with him he disturbs me—more than disturbs: contorts, dislocates, everything jumbles in my mind and goes out of focus. I haven't said anything about it before because I don't want to upset my children. The young are so fragile. But it has been very hard for me to bear and it's getting worse. It was particularly bad this morning, when I felt perfectly composed until I went to sit beside him. He must have grown up in a more chaotic state than I realised. I've sometimes felt since his illness that he has never had more than a rudimentary grasp of how a society such as ours functions. He isn't able to put all the bits and pieces together and make something intelligible out of it. He has always been rather like a child sent out on an errand who has no road sense and doesn't understand traffic signals, but now there seems to be a positive orientation towards disorder.'

'Whereas you see society as a well-lit stage, with stability, law and order as the furniture and props which enable people to move about confidently and pursue their aims?'

'Is there anything wrong with that?' Florence had not expected anything quite so succinct from her sister.

'Isn't there always turmoil, but at certain times and in certain places we are less aware of it?'

'I might have known it would be hopeless talking to you. You have always been subversive.'

Sophia, face cupped in hands, regarded the marmalade pot with puzzled concern. 'I wonder where the lid has got to. Now, where did I last see it?' She was wearing a misty blue turtle-necked sweater surmounted by what looked to Florence to be a long grey sack with slits for arms and neck.

As she looked at her sister, Florence was aware of anger always simmering inside her, an anger which sometimes boiled up unaccountably. Ever since she could remember, Sophia had looked as if she had started late for an appointment the purpose of which she had already forgotten. It astonished Florence that despite this she had never actually come to grief. She recalled that years ago, when Sophia had given up her job as a silversmith in order to come and live in the cottage, she had said to Konrad, 'Not that I wish her any harm, but it does seem a perverseness in life that someone can take so many unwarrantable risks and never be any the worse for it.'

'That sounds as if you did want something to happen to her,' he had replied.

'I would just like her to know that actions have consequences.'

And yet, they were not unalike. There were times, brief flashes rather than occasions, when Florence was aware that at some level they understood each other perfectly. This was not a comforting insight.

'You need to do something with your hair,' she said. Hair was important to Florence, an index of health and general sanity. 'You live a very unorganised life and if you don't take yourself in hand you are going to end up one of those dotty old women who scarcely knows night from day, walking barefoot and living on herbs and nettle soup.'

Sophia licked the marmalade spoon.

'I'm not suggesting you dye your hair. But there are measures one can take. I had thought of having my hair dyed—just until all the strands have made up their mind what they're arriving at. But I've noticed it gives people such a bad colour when the hair is touched up and the skin is past that. So I compromise by running a comb through tea, which gives it a faint tobacco colour.'

Sophia said, 'And you will grow into a well-preserved old trout.'

These words haunted Florence long after Sophia had forgotten the image of a dotty, barefoot old woman. As she stumbled through the snow on her way to visit the Prentices, she was quite afraid she would come across a pond and see mirrored in its glassy surface a corseted grotesque so renovated that nothing remained of the original human person.

*   *   *

Thomas Challoner gave Frances a generous allowance and never enquired—nor was interested in—how she spent it. He was not, in fact, very interested in Frances, whom he found rather boring. This did not mean that he had no feeling for her; he was touched by her solitariness and apprehensive as to what would become of her. He had tried to encourage her to make friends with local people and it was thanks to his efforts that she had taken a part-time job in a local bookshop. In some ways his attitude to her was akin to his approach to certain books which, however worthy of respect and therefore to be absorbed dutifully, failed to kindle his imagination.

Today, however, Frances was claiming his attention on a trivial matter and Thomas, who thought a little triviality in Frances was no bad thing, set himself to oblige. She had bought a dress and had put it on for his consideration. 'I rushed in and got it yesterday while Nicholas was working through Florence's order. I'm not sure it's right now. What do you think?'

Thomas, aware that this was the standard female reaction to any article of clothing purchased, proceeded warily. 'The colour is good on you.' It was a bright orange, a colour Anita could never wear, which was presumably a bonus, since Anita would be the only other young woman present at lunch.

'You don't like the style?'

It had a sleeveless bodice with a dropped waistline and a lot of fluting and other paraphernalia in the skirt. Thomas thought it was the kind of dress in which chorus girls would have performed the Charleston.

'A bit fussy here and there,' he hazarded.

'I could take the bow off and the ribbon.'

'Perhaps you could wear the ribbon round your neck?' She looked so bony and, although this was the fashion, he judged that her purpose on this occasion was to attract Nicholas rather than to compete with Anita. He could not imagine that even a man so remote as Nicholas would be attracted by a display of skin and bone.

'I think a long scarf would be better,' she said.

'There was a rather threadbare bead shawl in the dressing-up trunk at one time. I remember Margery wore it when we had a fancy-dress party here one Christmas and she was a Spanish dancer.' He thought the shawl would cover the sharp-boned shoulders as well as the neck and breast-bone. Thomas liked softly rounded shoulders on a woman.

'We're going to look in the dressing-up trunk,' Frances called to Andrew who was playing football in the hall with Jasper; but Andrew went on lecturing Jasper, who could not be made to understand that it was only in rugby that one was allowed to run with the ball.

The dressing-up trunk revealed as well as the shawl a long black chiffon scarf which Frances declared to be the very thing. 'But I can't wear it smelling of moth balls. Do you think it will disintegrate if I wash it?'

'You have enough time to find out.' He turned the gossamery shawl over in his hands. 'You don't like this?'

She looked at the shawl and then, putting a hand on his sleeve, said, 'Not on me. I'm not as beautiful as Margery was.' She went away to wash the scarf.

Thomas sat on the trunk with the shawl across his knees and wished that Margery were here with him. Never a day passed but her loss presented itself in one way or another: the longing for company on a forest walk, the need to talk of Jonathan, a household problem, a joke too salty to share with Frances, a worry over Andrew. 'If only Margery were here,' he would say with many different intonations. Usually, her loss took the form of a dull ache, a feeling of something not in its place in the house, an ingredient missing in the fare life offered. But at this moment, the pain was as sharp as on the day she died and with it came the panic when he thought of the days, months, perhaps years ahead. He had managed well, friends assured him, but now, sitting here in the dusty attic, it seemed to him that he had not gained more than a foothold in that barren land in which he now found himself.

He was aware that Margery would not wish him to give way to despair, so as soon as he had regained his composure he folded the shawl carefully and replaced it in the trunk.

Far below, he heard voices, and going to the small window he saw Nicholas hoisting Andrew on to a pony, Jasper cavorting around them. As he led the pony towards the forest, Frances came out on to the path, waving. The scene sparkled with vigour and gaiety as snow scenes can when the sun comes out. Thomas had watched Nicholas's mild flirtation with Frances with detached amusement. It had taken him only a short time to recognise in Nicholas the kind of man who shies away from serious emotional engagement. But now, seeing the three of them in the tableau so typical of a young family at Christmas, he thought how natural it was and how superfluous his own presence.

He went slowly down the stairs to join Frances in the kitchen. As he entered the room she was testing the iron. She saw that he was in command of himself again and was proud of him, always so steady and upright, even though sometimes it seemed to her that he was like a soldier under indefinite sentence. She knew that he would have considered it a betrayal of Margery had he 'made a poor fist' of his widowerhood. She had wrapped the scarf in a towel to get as much moisture as possible out before ironing it, and she made a business of unrolling it to cover any slight awkwardness between them.

'Would you care for a coffee?' Thomas asked. 'A Gaelic coffee, perhaps?'

She said 'Why not?' with rather edgy enthusiasm.

While he made the coffee she separated the scarf from the towel carefully as if it were something very precious.

'It's all right so far,' she said, spreading the flimsy material out over the ironing board. 'I've got the iron at a low heat. Say a prayer for me.'

She was flushed and this animated her face. He thought that perhaps he had not said enough prayers for her. She had come to regard this house as her home while Margery was alive and there had been no doubt then of her need, a lonely, unhappy girl, starved of affection. The death of Jonathan had drawn her closer to them; she had grieved as if one of the family. Although she was rather too intense for his liking, he had accepted her as a daughter for whom he had as much responsibility as for Andrew.

Now, looking around the kitchen, not as homely as when Margery presided, but clean and well stocked, it occurred to him that there had been a shift in their relationship so gradual he had not noticed it; the need had become his and it was Frances on whom the burden of care lay.

'I nearly made a mistake yesterday,' Frances said. 'It was on the tip of my tongue to mention Konrad—as if I'd met him, I mean.'

'Yes, I slipped up, too.'

'It's odd, don't you think? Nicholas out with the pony this morning, and all of us going to Christmas lunch. It's as if they didn't want to know what was happening.'

Thomas, not much minded to judge his neighbours, said, 'Mmh. We don't know any of them very well, do we?'

'But it's better to be aware, isn't it?' she persisted, bearing down rather hard on the flimsy scarf. 'Even if it's something you're not going to like, it's better to know.'

'It may be better to be prepared,' he said

slowly. 'But it doesn't lessen the pain.'

'That's what I meant,' she said, with a little less conviction. How mismanaged it seemed that Margery should have been the one taken and he, so little fitted to deal with the complexities of human behaviour and emotions, should be the survivor.

'You're happy about going over there for lunch?' he asked, feeling this was the most he could do by way of probing her feelings for Nicholas.

'We couldn't not go, could we?' she said.

'We could say we had succumbed to this deadly virus.'

She draped the scarf round her neck while she folded the ironing board. 'If we didn't go, we should have Florence round here ministering to us. She was very taken with you.'

Thomas held up a hand in mock horror. 'Don't say that. Even in jest, don't say that.'

Frances went upstairs to change. Thomas, washing up the coffee cups, reflected that not the least of the things she had done for him was to save him from such as Florence. He was a proud man whose independence was important to him. The possibility that Frances might go—indeed should be encouraged to go whenever the time was right for her—leaving him to become the object of pity and calculation was more than distasteful, it was frightening. There was

Andrew to consider. He had known several men who had made disastrous second marriages for the sake of their children. For a moment, as he dried the cups and trod in Jasper's lunch bowl, he felt threatened as never before.

*   *   *

'Our history teacher says all explorers are a little mad,' Andrew said as Nicholas led the pony into what Andrew imagined to be a Himalayan glade.

'It helps,' Nicholas said soberly. The history teacher had been joking, but the face which Nicholas turned to the wood was striated with lines that owed more to anxiety than humour. 'At least, I don't think it would be something you'd do to prove you were a fairly ordinary sort of person.'

He had thought only this morning as he was shaving that the eyes which started out of the thin face were too bright—not the brightness of expectancy, either, more desperation. But then, the cottage was small and there was a tree right up against the bathroom window.

'Have you been to the Amazonian rain forests?' Andrew asked.

'No. I try to steer clear of jungle and forest as far as I can. I need space. Explorers aren't necessarily brave. I'm not even at ease here in your airy wood.'

Andrew, for whom the forest was a place of refuge, said, 'I'd like to explore the rain forests.' He rubbed the pony's shoulder, which was the colour of coconut matting and just as prickly. The mane was flaxen and so were the eyelashes, which protruded stiff as the bristles of a toothbrush above the dark, liquid eyes.

It seemed to Nicholas as he led the boy on the pony through the wood that this was not Andrew but another, long-lost child from whom he needed something rather badly—only he was not sure what. It was a very long time since he had been sure of anything. The boy on the pony was wise in his own fashion because, being at his beginning, he was master of the here and now; whereas Nicholas had become one of those lean and foolish knights who go on quests and after many arduous adventures come to realise that they have forgotten what it is they quested. He said to Andrew, humbly, as if he needed to know, 'Why do you want to be an explorer?'

'But you must know.' The boy was surprised.

'I did once. Perhaps you could remind me.'

'I'd be able to go where I want and do what I want when I want, of course. And get lost without people making a fuss.'

'But do you know what you want?'

'Well, I don't want to go to school, for a start.'

'But what do you want from your exploring—can you tell me?'

Andrew wrinkled up his nose so that his cheekbones touched the big round glasses. 'I won't know that till I get wherever it is, will I? I mean, if I knew what it was before I got there, it wouldn't be worth exploring, would it? It would be like one of those treasure hunts where someone goes and tells you where to look.'

'And when you got there, and you knew, do you think it would have been worth it?'

'It depends. Grandad took us to France for the day last year and it was just like England, streets and shops. They even had the same T-shirts. I think what I'd do would be to search for something—a lost city, that sort of thing. If it had been lost for centuries it would be bound to be different, wouldn't it? And there wouldn't be any people.' No people was obviously a bonus.

They went on in silence for a little while and then Andrew said, 'And you'd be free. I mean, you're never free here, are you? There's always someone on at you about something.' He played with the pony's tangled mane, making up his mind to speak. 'I'm not good at games, you see. Do you think that would stop me?'

'I shouldn't think so. Unless you go in for the sort of thing where you have to be first.'

Again they were silent until Andrew said, bending down as if speaking for the pony's ear alone, 'And there'd be no one to worry whether I was happy.'

Nicholas said, 'I don't know ...' He knuckled his forehead to no effect. 'I wish I could help you, but I don't really know any more than you. I've just covered more miles, that's all.'

'Could I come with you some time, when I'm a bit older?'

'We'll see.'

'I'd train and all that. I'm quite fit. I don't really need these glasses. It's just that it's easier to sort of work things out behind them.'

'No promises. You might want to do something different in a few years' time and I might ... well, one never knows. Promises are things which don't leave people free.'

Andrew sighed. 'Grandad tells me promises are meant to be kept.'

I go on and on searching, Nicholas thought, and all the time I get thinner and my eyes get wilder. It's as if I'm wearing myself away and one day there won't be anything of me at all except a pair of staring eyes.

'We're going in a circle, did you know?' Andrew asked politely. 'We've just passed the double oak again.'

'I hadn't noticed. I'm sorry.'

'Shall I walk the pony now?' Andrew was getting a little tired of just sitting, and cold as well.

Nicholas turned to help him down and he said, 'I can manage. It's not as if he's very tall.' But Nicholas was standing so near that he couldn't get down without pushing. For a moment, they remained still, looking at each other. Nicholas said, 'The one place we never see is what's at the back of our head. We don't see as far round as a lot of animals, and birds have a much more panoramic view. What I'm trying to say is—you don't think you would ever feel that you ought to explore what you have turned your back on?'

'I wouldn't have turned my back if I'd wanted to explore it, would I?' Andrew said primly.

'Yes, silly of me.' Nicholas stood back while Andrew scrambled down.

Andrew said, 'Shall I take you and show you the tawny owl's tree?'

*   *   *

Anita sat with her father while Florence helped Sophia to prepare for lunch. At half-past ten, Sophia relieved her.

'Where is Mother?' Anita asked.

'She is gone on a goodwill mission to the

Prentices.'

'But it's here that she's needed.'

'She needed to get out.' Sophia looked tired. 'What is more, I needed her to get out.'

'I could visit Terence this afternoon, if you'd like me to help you now.' As Sophia seemed unable to make up her mind about this, Anita said, 'Or perhaps you need me to get out as well?'

'If you wouldn't mind.' Sophia passed a hand across her eyes. 'I'm sorry, but I'm not good in the morning, nothing seems to function, brain included. The doctor says it's my heart that's not up to much.'

She would not normally have confided this, Anita guessed; that she did so was a mark of her extreme need to be rid of her guests.

Anita had the tact to go quickly. In a matter of minutes, a scarf bound round her shorn head, she was on her way to visit Terence. She, too, was glad to be on her own.

It was bitterly cold still, but bright and Anita found the clear, sharp air invigorating. It seemed her father walked with her as he had long ago on a perfect winter's day when she had felt light and new as the first snowdrop. It came to her more vividly than recollection, as though the two experiences had become one. She walked through a landscape itself made new, boundaries, barriers and paths all blotted out. She passed a signpost pointing with laid-back hilarity to a hamlet somewhere in the sky. She felt a tinge of regret when she saw the first house in the distance—Millionaires' Acre, Sophia had dubbed this area on the outskirts of the forest. The hurricane had stripped the houses of their protective cover and they now gazed baldly across their snow-covered lawns. Anita could imagine the owners fighting for the preservation of the forest as passionately as if their own dwellings had grown with the greenwood. The Carteret house was small in comparison with some of its neighbours, but it had an air of discreet wealth, each jewelled window radiating soft coloured lights. There was a big holly wreath hanging on the front door.

Anita felt rather like Elizabeth Bennet approaching the residence of the Bingleys to visit her sick, only not so well disposed to the sufferer. When she had telephoned to speak to Terence, messages had been relayed by Mrs. Carteret because 'he finds it difficult to speak'. The messages had related to Terence's BUPA membership and the steps to be taken to ensure the college was made sufficiently aware of the crippling nature of his injuries. He had not included any greetings to her—or Mrs. Carteret had not seen fit to pass them on; her tone had suggested that she held Anita to blame for Terence having set out on such a foolhardy expedition. 'One has to know the ways of the forest,' she had said, sounding like one of J. M. Barrie's more fey characters.

There were several children and a dog playing in the garden under the supervision of a young man whose chunkiness was beginning to turn to flab. From Sophia's description, Anita took him to be Mrs. Carteret's son. The whole group regarded her with the suspicion of the stranger peculiar to wealthy country-house owners. The son must be in his late twenties, Anita judged; which meant that Mrs. Carteret must be going on fifty. This was unlikely to inhibit Terence, provided she was personable and agreeable. Anita knocked on the front door and after a longish pause she was admitted by a round little woman with a cloud of ash-blonde hair and a face as soft as marshmallow. She held a glass of wine in one dimpled hand and didn't look as if she had been recently occupied in the kitchen.

'I hope you're not going to disturb him,' she said, examining Anita much as a wren might observe a hovering hawk from the shelter of a hedge. 'He's had a quiet morning so far.'

'She looked at me as if she thought I was going to dive into bed with you,' Anita said to Terence when they were alone. She noticed a glass of wine on the bedside table.

Terence looked anxious lest the idea should prove irresistible. Anita thought he resembled a panda with the black smudges round his eyes. 'There's small chance of that,' he said. 'I can't take a deep breath without feeling someone is at me with a branding iron.'

'Really as bad as that?' She regarded his chest judicially as if at any moment she might poke to verify the truth of this assertion.

'I'm not joking.'

'But a branding iron? Having quite an effect on you, isn't it, this forest retreat? Do you feel you've slipped into another century, perhaps?'

'I could have punctured a lung, that's what should be worrying you.'

'There'd be blood, wouldn't there? Did you gash crimson all over the snow?'

'What are you so edgy about? And why have you got your hair bundled up as if you'd just come out of the bath?'

'You want to know?' She unwrapped the scarf.

Terence gave a sharp intake of breath and screeched with agony. 'You look dreadful,' he said when he could speak. 'Like one of those women who collaborated with the Nazis.' The idea seemed to waken unpleasant associations in his mind. 'What have you been up to?'

'I thought I needed a change.'

'You're not the same person.'

'That, too.'

'Just what has been happening in that cottage?'

She got up and walked around the room, picking up ornaments, opening the wardrobe, pulling out drawers. 'It's a comfortable room, isn't it? She didn't stash you away in the attic, did she? Warm, central heating working nicely, no electricity failure. I expect they generate their own. Lots of pleasant smells. Telephone so that you can have a chat to anyone you might want to speak to. Comfortable bed, good springs ...' She made as if to test the springs and he bared his teeth in a grimace of anguish. 'All right, all right, I don't intend to do it. But you have to admit you chose a good spot to incapacitate yourself.'

'Incapacitate myself? I was mown down by a flying toboggan. You don't seem to understand that I am racked with pain. I never knew what that meant before...'

'Actually, it means stretched. You haven't been stretched, crumpled rather. I'm sick of all this self-pity. What about me? Sleeping alone in that icy bed.' She put her face close to his, mouth to mouth.

'Anita, please!'

'It's the one thing you can do.'

'What's left of your hair is tickling my nose. If I cough it's sheer agony.'

'It can't be as bad as that. You must be doped to the eyeballs.'

'The doctor didn't leave that many painkillers. He wasn't very sympathetic when Mrs. Carteret phoned for more. He's spending his Christmas looking after people who have been poisoned by your mother and he's obviously happy that someone connected with her should suffer.'

There was a little bowl of snowdrops beside the glass of wine. 'A nice touch,' Anita said. 'From Mr. Carteret, are they?'

'She's a divorcée.'

'Ah, the poor soul!'

'She has been very kind to me.'

'You're probably the best thing to have come her way in a long time.'

'This wasn't an assignation. I don't need to go to those lengths.'

Anita stood by the window, trying to gain some control over herself. A short time ago she had felt a new-formed, almost ethereal creature. Now, within minutes of coming into this room, she was subject to the impatience and resentment which Terence only too often aroused in her.

'You have a cruel, bad-tempered face.' He meant her to pay for the pain and inconvenience he had suffered. 'I never noticed it before.'

'Probably because you never notice anyone but yourself.'

'A little bit of sympathy would be welcome. But then you've never had any patience with sickness.'

'I sat up with you when you had flu so badly last winter.'

'Only because you said I was so restless you couldn't sleep. It's been a revelation to me, being nursed here.'

'If it's revelation you want, I dare say I could provide one.'

She was standing over him, glinting eyes and flushed cheeks signalling one of the outbursts of temper which he usually liked to precipitate. This time, however, he had failed to calculate the risk to himself. He tried to shrink away from her and gave a whimper of pain.

She saw that he was genuinely alarmed. Terence's emotions were so seldom genuine that this was a moment to be cherished. Her anger evaporated as suddenly as it had flared up. 'We've never been very good at looking after each other, have we?'

'You're hardly the maternal sort, are you?' he said sullenly.

'Oh well, if it's mothering you want ...' But that, of course, was exactly what he wanted and always had. She turned away and sat down on the window-seat. Terence, who was very dependent on her but did not

164

want to be the one to break off hostilities, indulged in a few agonised intakes of breath.

Anita said, rubbing the pane of glass that her breath had misted over, 'I'm sorry you've had this little upset. Is there anything I can do?'

'Little upset! That's a fine way of putting it. But then you have always buggered things up at crucial moments and then made light of it. In the hurricane, if you remember—'

'Oh, not that again! That's ancient history now.'

' ... you and your mother were holidaying in Lake Garda while I was trying to get a tree out of the bedroom.'

'I don't believe you were even there when the tree came down. I think you were sleeping with Thelma Armitage.'

Terence was so outraged that he tried to haul himself up in the bed and knocked over the bowl of snowdrops. 'For God's sake mop this up before it leaves a permanent mark on the carpet.'

'I'm sorry.' Anita pummelled her cheeks with clenched fists. 'I didn't mean to bring up Thelma Armitage. I wanted us to be different this morning. I wanted ...' She could find no words to justify the ten years they had indifferently sheltered each other.

'If you don't mop this up I'm going to have to call her,' Terence said, gesturing in the direction of the telephone, which was out

165

of his reach.

'Oh sod the carpet! You haven't even asked ...' She stopped, shocked to realise that she had been about to use her father as a counter in this shabby quarrel. She got up briskly. 'Right. Where's your flannel.'

'Not the flannel!'

But she was already mopping the carpet. 'It's only water. It shouldn't leave a mark unless the carpet is dirty.' She tossed the flannel unwrung into the hand-basin.

'It will smell if you don't wring it out,' Terence said pettishly.

Anita put the snowdrops in fresh water. 'There. I'd better get back now. You seem to be quite well cared for. You'll have to wait until after Christmas for your present.'

'There are one or two things I'll need from the flat when I go to hospital. I've made a list. And there's the car to be seen to and ...'

'The AA can do that.'

'If you want to risk it. Your present is in it. I'll tell you about the things in the flat next time you come. You may be in a better mood then.' He looked at her resentfully. 'You haven't explained about your hair.'

'If you must know, I made it into four plaits and then cut them off.'

'Oh, well, if you don't want to tell me.' He could look very appealing when he chose but there was a residual pettiness in him which tended more and more to sour his

166

expression. Anita touched the puckered mouth. 'You'll have to watch that.' She bent forward and kissed him on the lips. 'I've missed you. I've missed you so much.'

'It's not much fun for me, not knowing what you're getting up to.'

'It's distrusting each other so much that has kept us together,' she said, smoothing the curly yellow hair back from his brow. 'Don't suffer too much.'

*   *   *

Now they were all out of the cottage, the intruders. It was only two days that they had been here, yet it seemed weeks that their restlessness had disturbed the hearth. Tobias stretched full length in front of the sitting-room fire in an ecstasy of warmth and peace, the brown face for once eyeless.

A great quiet had descended over all. Beyond the window of Konrad's room there was no movement. The honeysuckle twigs which had come free of their burden of snow formed a delicate pattern on which the sun shed a geometric grace. Konrad and Sophia, their fingers intertwined, were like figures in a painting from which the frame has been removed.

*   *   *

The sky, which had been blue, was yellowish now. Clouds were forming again, high at present. Through gaps in the trees the unfamiliar landscape stretched for miles. Florence could see a clump of trees on a hill. Before the hurricane, they would have been as finely tapered as a head of hair, but now, after five years, they were still in horrible disarray, the apex shattered while grisly tufts stood out around it, as if a giant hand had reached in twisting and turning.

The snow was hard and walking was very tiring. Florence was aware that she had overtaxed her strength. She rested her back against the trunk of a tree. There was utter stillness.

She tried to warm herself with thoughts of families gathered together, drinking mulled wine, exchanging perfunctory gallantries under mistletoe, putting the last touches to the brandy butter, children clamouring to open presents. But the picture, so precious to her, seemed strangely remote, not only in place but in time. When had it been, this perfect Christmas with which she was so familiar? As she searched for it in her mind she seemed to be tearing at a wonderfully wrapped package which contained a series of boxes getting smaller and smaller until eventually there was nothing but a piece of ice.

How had it come about that she was here,

alone, banished from the good fellowship? Left out. She had never before been left out. She had made it her business to ensure that she had a proper role. All her life her position had been central—daughter, wife, mother; she had always had contempt for those who lived on the fringes of other people's lives: spinsters, maiden aunts, confirmed widows. Suddenly, she put back her head and howled.

Anita, coming briskly down the track, was startled by this cry as of an animal deserted by the herd.

'Whatever is it now?' she asked, when she had satisfied herself that her mother was not having a fit.

Florence, who had no wish to speak of the desolation she had experienced, said, 'They were most ungracious, those Prentices. I should have gone to Mass.'

'You would never have made it to the town. Wasn't last night's struggle enough for you?'

'And how was lover boy?'

'I think we'd better save our breath. It's nearly half-past twelve and the Challoner lot are coming at one o'clock.'

A party, Florence thought. It was something for which to prepare and she was grateful for this, but there was no joy in the thought. And she knew, as she groomed herself for the occasion, that something had

169

been taken away that would not be restored to her.

★ ★ ★

He thought he could hear the ice piano again, each note distinct as a pearl; but now, underneath it, scarcely audible to the human ear, he began to be aware of another sound not composed of isolated notes, a sound that was like the faint whisper of a calm sea as it meets the shore, the breath of wind in the trees, the humming of bees on a summer evening, but was none of these things.

★ ★ ★

'Terence is a lecturer at a teacher training college,' Florence explained for the benefit of Thomas Challoner, seeking to give Terence what respectability could honestly be accorded him. She had seated herself by the lamp in the sitting-room and the light played softly on the curls which dressed the top of her head like a crown of lamb. 'A stable occupation is something to be thankful for nowadays.'

'It's not a stable occupation,' Anita said. 'The structure of education changes every time the Secretary of State has a bad dream. The only stable thing is to be on a radio chat show.'

'I should see if you can help in the kitchen,' Florence advised.

Anita went into the hall, where she met Frances carrying bread sauce. Nicholas was uncorking a bottle of wine presented by Thomas. Frances said, 'I like your hair,' by which she meant she was pleased that Anita's glory had been shed. Her own dark hair hung loose around the shoulders of her brilliant dress. Anita, unadorned as an exclamation mark in her green sheath, felt her throat constrict as she looked at Frances.

Nicholas said, 'It makes you look younger.'

Anita went into the kitchen. 'If you want someone to carve, I'm ready to start on my brother,' she said to Sophia.

In the sitting-room, Florence was saying to Thomas, 'One has to be patient and tolerant, I realise that. It's natural and fitting for young people to toss ideas about and experiment with different life styles. For older people to join in is just pathetic—don't you think?—like displaying ageing bodies in teenage clothes and kicking up their poor old limbs in the latest dance. The young don't need us to identify with them—they can get along quite well without our approval. Look at Tilly Pavener,' she said to Anita who had come back into the room.

'What about her?'

'Toiling off to Tibet and becoming a

Buddhist. And now her young have got over all that and settled down to a mainstream life in Putney and poor old Tilly and her Buddhism are just a burden to them.'

'Lunch is served, more or less,' Anita said.

Florence went into the dining-room talking about the necessity to age gracefully. In acknowledgement of this she had put on a billowy muslin tea-gown borrowed from the Chiswick theatre's wardrobe. Thomas, following in her wake, looked noble as though on his way to the scaffold and meaning to make a good end.

'Who was it who said how important it is to let go?' Florence asked, shaking out her napkin.

'Sophia,' Anita said. 'About an hour ago.'

'Someone else,' Florence snapped.

'I'm sure Nicholas spends a lot of time holding on.' Frances looked at Nicholas as he poured wine. 'I mean, to ropes and things.'

Thomas raised his glass. 'To our hostess.' He smiled at Sophia. She sat at one end of the table, he at the other. This arrangement had not pleased Florence but as she could not suggest anything more appropriate without giving offence she had consented to it. Now she saw that her forbearance had been well advised, for she was seated next to Thomas and although Sophia occupied the hostess's place she was unlikely to attract attention since she had chosen to remain in the grey sacking and looked muted as one of those sadly reflective women so beloved of Gwen John.

Andrew said, 'Can we feed the pony when we've finished this?'

'We'll have to find out who it belongs to, won't we?' Frances said to Sophia. 'He's obviously well cared for.' She was worried lest Andrew should invest too much in the pony. Florence thought it an impertinence to talk of 'we' as if staking a claim to family membership.

'P'raps some people brought him in a horse box and they've had a bad accident and died,' Andrew suggested hopefully.

'You, of course, must know so much about the forest and its people,' Florence said to Thomas. 'That silver grey couple were telling me how much work you do on behalf of the Commoners.'

'I keep an eye on the legal side.'

'And even if they are alive, I shouldn't think they'd ever find him now, with all this snow,' Andrew mused.

'Your practice was in London, wasn't it?' Florence asked. 'It must be so healing to get away from that frantic existence.'

Nicholas, who had contributed nothing to the conversation, poured more wine.

'Perhaps he came from Millionaires' Acre?' Anita suggested to Sophia.

'I rather doubt it. Most of their animals are as new as their cars.'

' ... hurtling to destruction with all the little management men clutching their briefcases and discussing computer systems.' Florence was talking rapidly, her colour high.

While Sophia was clearing the main course, Anita went upstairs to Konrad's room. He looked quiet and peaceful, his face free of stress. There is no one there any more, she thought.

*   *   *

He was, in fact, intensely there. All the sounds had come together into the one sound of a spinning top. The top belonged to his lost early childhood and he now saw it very clearly. It was green with crimson dragons curled around it and it had holes through which light flashed as it turned faster and faster until the sound ceased and the light became continuous.

*   *   *

When Anita returned to the dining-room Florence was talking about her love of the theatre. Anita picked up the bread sauce which had been overlooked and went into the kitchen, where Sophia was pouring brandy over the Christmas pudding. 'I don't care how we have this pudding,' she said wearily, 'but I expect Andrew would like to see it alight.'

'My mother is boring on about Mozart and Salieri now,' Anita said. 'Never mind that Mozart was given ten talents and returned them a thousandfold, it's the dreary moral question she's latched on to. She's obviously decided that Thomas is a model of virtue.'

'In some ways, he is,' Sophia said quietly. She struck a match and after one or two attempts the brandy caught alight. No one, least of all Andrew, who was gazing out of the window in the hope of catching sight of the pony, paid much attention. Florence was busy defending Salieri's right to make God aware of his dissatisfaction with the way awards and punishments were meted out.

Anita said, 'All this business about Salieri has been an absolute gift to second-rate people.'

'There are no second-rate people.' Florence accompanied this pronouncement with a generous gesture.

'The world is largely peopled by the second-rate, who don't make the most of what talents they have.'

'How many times have you returned your talent, then?' Florence demanded. 'You gave up that writing course when you took up with Terence.'

'Talking to you is like trying to have a discussion with a bird. You wheel away high up above the pull of consistency.'

'That's rather good.' Florence smiled tolerantly. 'You should be a writer, darling. But then you'd have to learn to spell.'

'I wonder why we have developed such a passion for precision,' Thomas improvised, hoping to introduce a subject that would give Florence less chance to scintillate. 'Take spelling, for example...'

'How can she talk such rubbish?' Anita grumbled to Sophia when they were in the kitchen making coffee.

'It's not all rubbish. She has always been in charge. Now she is talking of letting go.'

'She didn't mean that.'

'Perhaps not; but she is experimenting with the idea.'

Sophia had put coffee in the grinder; now, she stood staring at it, her face clouded. 'I'm sorry. I can't think how this works.'

Anita said gently, 'Among other things, it works by electricity.'

'How silly of me. I don't know what I'm doing,' Sophia said. Tears ran down her cheeks unchecked.

Anita said, 'I'll find some instant.' She went into the larder and when she returned Sophia was still standing in front of the coffee grinder, crying silently.

'Why don't you go upstairs,' Anita said. 'I can cope with this.'

'Yes, in a moment.' She made no attempt either to excuse or conceal her emotion, but waited for it to pass, standing with her hands resting loosely on the table, her head bowed. She is not like other people, Anita thought, used to the face which must conceal rather than reveal. She is the same inside as out. It made Sophia seem strange, formidable even, not entirely to be trusted, as if there must be some trick.

Nicholas opened the door, Frances behind him. 'I need to walk off that splendid meal,' he said to no one in particular. 'And Frances, too. So no coffee for us.'

'Do you mind?' Anita asked Sophia when Nicholas and Frances had collected their boots from the scullery and departed looking restrained, if not actually cross, as if on their way to perform a necessary duty imposed on them against their will.

'It's not for me to mind.'

'She's your neighbour.'

'Oh, Frances, you mean?'

'Well, I didn't mean Nicholas. He won't come to any harm.'

'He will just go away and climb another mountain, is that it?'

*　　*　　*

177

Frances stood by the kitchen window while coffee percolated. Her dressing gown fell open to reveal her nakedness and her feet were bare. Jasper sat beside her looking exceedingly glum. Every now and again he swallowed as if his throat were dry.

The big, high-ceilinged room, lit only by a lamp, was shadowy. But it was tears, not shadows, that blurred Frances's face and tempered the severity that gave her features something of the fixity of an icon. Now, no longer becalmed, different emotions chased across her face with the unpredictability of an April day.

Jasper moaned.

'Drink your water,' Frances commanded.

He refused to take his eyes from her. She bent down and picked up his bowl, holding it for him. Hastily, he licked the tears from her face before drinking from the bowl. Her hair fell forward across his furrowed brow. 'It's no use getting yourself in a state,' she said. 'What's done is done.' She shook her hair back, her face transformed by exultant gaiety.

Thus Nicholas saw her as he came cautiously into the room. Jasper growled deep in his chest. 'It's all right,' Frances soothed both man and beast.

But it was not the dog that had startled Nicholas. To someone who prided himself on passing through, like the American

178

Indians, leaving the landscape as he found it, the change in Frances was deeply disturbing. Yet had he not wanted to touch and see what happened?

'Sit down,' she said. 'He won't bite you.'

'I'm not so sure. There can't be a dwelling within five miles' radius where he hasn't made his displeasure known.'

She herself had made a surprising amount of noise. Like a creature under enchantment, who must incorporate the fullness of experience in one encounter, she had passed with rapidity through the stages of love-making, nervous stiffness and gritty determination merging into playfulness and provocation followed by a startlingly sudden surrender. Her passionate response had been relayed by a series of unearthly howls from Jasper on the landing. Nicholas looked at her warily. She was pouring coffee and crying steadily. 'It's all right,' she assured him. 'It's only that I don't seem to be able to stop.'

There seemed no doubt that from her point of view it was all right. Her tears were like rain in sunlight.

Nicholas bent his head over the cup, uncertain how to proceed. The uncertainty was perilous.

'I'm happy,' she assured him, wiping away the tears, her fingers lingering on her cheeks, the feel of her flesh new to her. She seemed charmed as if she had just had her ears pierced, eagerly contemplating the more exotic adornments she could now display.

'I'm glad,' he said drily.

'No, really, I'm happy.' Her forefinger traced the line of his cheekbone and rested on his lips. 'I'm happy, Nicholas.'

He flinched and she said softly, 'What is it?'

'It's the sort of person I am. I should have warned you. I'm not the confiding type—and I'm not a settler, or any of the things that go with being a settler, such as reliable, patient, faithful to a particular place or plot or person.'

'But that's the sort of person you're not. You do it all the time—in your books, when you're interviewed. Do you realise that? You always paint a picture of what you're not.' She spoke very gently because she was going to help him to a more positive attitude. 'Whereas . . .' She reached out and took his hand, turning it palm upwards. 'Shall I tell you what I see?' She glowed with the tender desire to please.

He snatched his hand away. 'Frances, I'll be leaving here after Boxing Day.'

'Yes, I know there isn't much time to talk.' She composed herself to listen, her shining regard fixed at a point between his eyes. This was disastrous: he had not intended there to be much in the way of talk. How to explain that what to her represented a beginning

180

was, in fact, the end? He was not good at explaining; his previous affairs had not necessitated it.

She cajoled, 'Why so solemn?' The intense grey eyes had learnt to tease.

'I don't suppose you could leave here,' he said. He had intended this as a statement made with a firmness only lightly tempered by regret. It came out as a question.

'No,' she agreed, almost absently, as if this were not an issue.

He was nonplussed. 'If I have to go and you have to stay, I don't quite see where that gets us, do you?' He was conceding something with everything he said.

The wind had dislodged a few autumn leaves from the pile of logs in the scullery and now they skittered across the floor. Frances leant towards Nicholas. Her thin body glimpsed in the opening of the dressing gown was more erotic than when she was stripped. In the light of the lamp, the flesh had a dusky bloom which made his fingers itch. The dog came forward, snarling. Nicholas said, 'We'd better go back upstairs.'

The house was cold and the temperature was dropping as the sun went down in a spume of crimson. They sat side by side on the bed, the duvet wrapped around them. She nestled close to him, cheek resting against his. 'I have to stay here for Andrew's

sake. But that needn't matter because you'll
want to travel to places I probably couldn't
go to even if I was free to travel.' Although
she spoke tentatively there was no doubt that
she was giving him permission for a few away
trips. Her fingers ran lightly over his body.

He said brusquely, 'And we should go on
like that indefinitely. Is that what you had in
mind?'

She was still as an animal suddenly
scenting danger. He should have finished it
then, but he wanted to extract some kind of
submission from her and let the moment
pass. She said, 'Only for a few years, until
Andrew is older. You wouldn't...'

'Never mind about me. Hasn't it ever
occurred to you that you have a life of your
own to live?'

'But how do I know this isn't it?'

'It's not something you can let other
people decide for you.'

'But other people do decide things. I
couldn't leave Thomas and Andrew.' She
eased her hand on the nape of his neck,
coaxing. He thrust her away, and getting up
went to the window. Ice was forming on the
inside of the pane. She followed him,
tripping over the edge of the duvet. He was
at once upset and pleased by her agitation.

'Thomas has been so good to the boy, but
he's not domesticated; he couldn't manage
on his own—I don't suppose he'd be allowed

182

to. Some busybody would complain to Social Services. You do see that, don't you?'

He said impatiently, 'The boy could go to boarding school.'

She drew in her breath. In the frosty light her eyes glinted sharp as broken glass. 'His mother leaves him, his father commits suicide, his grandmother dies; I come along for a while and then tire of it. So, pack him off to boarding school. That seems fair to you?'

'Life isn't fair.'

'Andrew is not going to boarding school,' she said on a rising note. 'I have promised him.'

'How very young you are.' He put a finger beneath her chin and saw the pulse that throbbed in her throat. 'You see things in black and white.'

She jerked her head to one side. 'Some things are black and white. People just blur them when they get older because it's more convenient not to see too clearly.'

'Well, it's no business of mine. I merely suggest you're throwing your life away.'

'On people, though—not on desert sands and a few moth-eaten camels.'

There was a long silence. It was as if something they had wanted to contain had escaped into the room. She said, 'I'm sorry, but you have to admit you're not all that realistic yourself. You go travelling in search of a place or primitive people which will reveal your true identity, or some such piffle.'

'Don't tell me, let me guess. While all the time it is waiting for me here at home, where I started, or some such piffle.'

'There's no need to be angry just because it's your life we're talking about now.'

'Of course I'm angry. Who do you think you are to talk to me like this? What have you made of your life so far?'

She said with the dignity of a school prefect, 'I've accepted obligations.'

'Obligations!' He picked up his trousers and began to dress. 'You've found a bolt-hole.'

'Obligations, Nicholas.' She darted in front of him, trying to distract him from his purpose. 'What are you going to do about your mother when your father dies?'

He pulled his sweater over his head and said, his voice muffled, 'My mother is well able to look after herself.'

'Not for half an hour, I'd guess.' She plucked at his sleeve. 'It's your mother that's your problem isn't it, Nicholas? I'd help you deal with it.'

'You would do what?' His face was white as salt.

'I'd be willing to take care of her as well as Thomas and Andrew.'

'And what do you think they would have

184

to say about that?'

'If it didn't suit them they'd have to make their own arrangements.'

Nicholas, looking into her upturned face, saw her more clearly than he usually observed other people. Although she was pleading with him, he was aware of her strength. One day, perhaps not far distant, she would become a forthright, uncompromising woman who would give more than it might be comfortable to receive. 'You and my mother wouldn't get on,' he said. 'You're both formidably capable.'

'I'm capable, she's not.' Suddenly her store of energy was exhausted. She slumped on to the bed, crumpled face thrust in hands. 'I don't think I can make it back to Sophia's. You'll have to apologise for me.'

'What do you imagine they'll think if I come back alone and say that?'

'What they're thinking anyway.' She brushed the back of her hand across her eyes. 'Does it matter what they think? I don't care about anything but you. Oh, Nicholas, what have I done to spoil things? What have I said?'

He screwed up his face, unexpectedly touched, but she thought he winced at the banality of the appeal and said, 'If you feel you need to explain, you could say I proposed to you and you turned me down.'

For a moment, no longer than a heartbeat,

and yet it seemed as if it was for ever, he saw this offer she had made not as something ridiculous, but as if it were arrival at the end of a journey, the glad recognition of a place long sought, a gated city. But gates close at night and cities have walls. He hesitated, his eyes already seeking a more distant horizon.

Frances said, 'Or you could just say we walked too far into the forest and got lost.'

★   ★   ★

'It's snowing quite heavily,' Nicholas said gratefully. 'I thought Frances should go home since we passed the house on our walk.'

'What will happen to the pony?' Andrew demanded.

Anita tapped her teeth with a fingernail. 'That's a point.'

Oh, to hell with the pony! thought Florence, who had spent an exhausting afternoon playing in the snow with Andrew and Thomas and the pony.

'He can go in my shed,' Thomas offered.

'And I can lead him there.'

'No, I think you should ride him.' Thomas said this quietly as if having given careful consideration to the matter, but there was no doubting his authority and the boy did not argue.

Florence was about to offer tea before the

party set off when she saw that Sophia was standing half-way down the stairs.

'I think you had better come,' Sophia said.

Florence's mouth popped open and her face collapsed like an empty pea pod. Anita put an arm round her mother's shoulders. Nicholas came behind her, an equerry's distance apart.

Thomas said, 'Don't worry about us. We'll see ourselves out.'

Florence stumbled on the first step; after that she negotiated the stairs as carefully as a blind person.

'We haven't said goodbye to Tobias,' Andrew said.

'You'll see him again soon.' Thomas wound a scarf round the boy's neck and tucked it in his waterproof jacket.

'Where've they all gone?'

'It's where we're going we have to think about. Have you got all your presents? We can put them in these two bags and the pony will carry them.'

'It's not anywhere nice where they've gone,' Andrew said, resigned to answering himself.

Thomas opened the door. There was no wind and the snow fell soft as moulting feathers as they moved into the darkness.

When the door had closed behind them, Tobias came and sat by the sitting-room fire, erect, paws between haunches. The candle in the window, the greenery arranged beneath a little statue of the Virgin, gave a gentle air of festivity, the awareness of a nativity.

*   *   *

Sophia had not drawn the curtains over the window and the room was so dimly lit that they could see the lacy pattern of falling snow. Firelight flickered on a wall. Everywhere movement, except here where Konrad lay.

Anita held one of his hands, Florence the other. Sophia and Nicholas stood at the foot of the bed. There was no rhythm of breathing now, only an occasional breath like an afterthought. The face was peaceful. Each of the faces in the semi-circle around him was briefly touched by that sense of the fullness of life which comes with its completion.

Some time after the last breath, Florence kissed the calm brow and made the sign of the cross. She said drily, 'I can't pray.' Anita put out her hand and closed the eyes. Sophia went to the chest of drawers and drew out a napkin.

Later, in the kitchen, Anita said, 'The undertaker will never get here in this.'

Sophia said, 'I can do what is necessary, if one of you will help me.'

There was silence while Anita and Nicholas looked at Florence. Then Nicholas turned and went out of the room with Sophia.

Florence remained standing by the window watching the snow mounting on the ledge. After several minutes, she said, 'Tomorrow I shall want an explanation of that boy with the dancing bear.'

CHAPTER FOUR

The house seemed full of Konrad. They all noticed it in their own way.

Florence discovered that it was no longer possible to keep him at bay. He was not out there, he was within her. And much, much younger than she, in his prime. He had such energy—not the energy which is dissipated, as was hers, in constant busyness, but the energy which is a fact of nature, as primitive as a wayside spring. Once, she had thought to drink from that spring.

When they were children, Sophia had run away once or twice a week—she had called it having an adventure. This had aroused uncharacteristic passion in their mother and father. Florence, who would have liked the attention but not the experience of stepping beyond the controls, had listened at night to her sister recounting her adventures and had envied her. 'You should come, too,' Sophia had said. But Florence had refused. When they were older, Sophia had said, 'A moonlit night beckons, an unlocked door invites. You should say yes to life.' It was the first time Florence had heard this phrase, now sadly shopsoiled, and she had always regarded her sister as its originator. In her own way, Florence had since said yes to life on a number of occasions, but always in carefully controlled situations where consequences could be calculated and risks limited; she had, in fact, become something of an expert in risk limitation. The problem with Sophia was that she never sought to control situations to which she said yes. When Florence taxed her with this she had quoted Rilke, ' "Let life have its way; life knows best." '

'I don't know about Rilke,' Florence had retorted. 'But my experience has been that life needs constant pokes and nudges and the occasional knee in the privates to stimulate action.'

'You see living as a masculine function?'

'I don't see much chance of it without a man.'

She had expected Konrad's energy to transform the external world for her. The external world was where Florence's hope lay. For her, the symbol was the reality; she really believed in the hidden valley, the lost city, the magic mountain. Konrad had never understood this. He didn't like travel and had no wish to go abroad. He, who had seemed so foreign, who was to have been the gateway to a more richly coloured world, had turned out to be totally lacking in imagination, rooted in the everyday of life. She had taxed him with this.

'Why can't you go in search of places to paint?' she had said. 'It's all out there—we should go to Venice, the Vienna Woods, the Taj Mahal'—how she longed to be one of those who referred to it casually as 'the Taj'—'the rose-red city half as old as time...'

'All fantasy,' he had shrugged. 'You and Nicholas are like blind people: you dream of fantastic places, Nicholas goes in search of them. You never see what is before your eyes.'

'I couldn't settle for this being all there was,' she had retorted contemptuously, making a Chekhovian gesture to indicate the smallness of Chiswick.

'All!' He had been genuinely amazed. 'But it is so strange, all around you, don't you see?'

There had been nothing in the way he had said this of the wonder which she associated with strangeness, rather a kind of terror. His paintings suggested he was unable to walk down a street in the assurance that the scene would stay in place until he reached the object of his outing, the pillar-box on the corner.

'If that's how you see things, no wonder you don't want to travel,' she had commented, on viewing one painting. 'Each time you turn your head you expect to see everything rearranged.'

He had been excited and clapped his hands and said he had not known she understood this.

'I don't understand,' she had shouted. 'It's all nonsense—worse, madness.' It had been after this that she had complained about the number of paintings in the house. 'If you wanted a woman who could live in an art gallery, you shouldn't have married me.' This had touched him. 'I hate the galleries, too,' he had said humbly and after that the paintings gradually, over a period of time, disappeared.

Yet, although she saw madness in his paintings, he himself had seemed massively calm, a great rock against which all the anger and hysteria generated by Florence and Anita broke in harmless clouds of spray. 'He is there,' she had told herself. 'He completes the picture.' She had become reconciled to seeing this as his role in the family. But now, in those uncomfortable moments of clarity which can come with the grey of dawn, she saw that it was he who had held their world in being. It seemed that the terror had purged him of the small anxieties, the petty vexations which grind down with the years. Never had Konrad appeared to be ground down. Nor did he seem to have any sense of oppression; whatever had happened to him in his early years, he had no idea of himself as a victim, no one whom he sought to blame, no urge to punish. She had a picture of him, as she lay watching the sun begin to bruise the ashen sky. She saw him seated by the window of their suburban sitting-room, gazing benignly over the mundane architectural chaos of Chiswick. His big head tilted sideways, the eyes little pouches of humour, the mouth composed as if a jest had recently escaped his lips, he looked not so much as if he felt at home in his world, but as if he had come to terms with its foreignness. A woman came into the room and Florence waited, with a thrill of fear and awe, to see herself walk quietly to the window and take her place opposite Konrad. They would talk as they had never talked before. And then the woman, who had seated herself, turned to the light and Florence saw that it was her sister, Sophia.

'Would you like your breakfast in bed?' Sophia asked.

'Certainly not. I have a lot to say and I would prefer to say it when I am up and dressed.'

★   ★   ★

Anita, wan as the day, stopped at the turn of the stairs, startled by the strong sweetness of hyacinth. And there below in the hall were hyacinths and crocuses released from their dark store, and winter jasmine wet with melted snow. Something twisted inside her, like the start of menstruation. She sat huddled on the stairs, hands clasping her elbows, instinctively protecting her body. Through the window she could see the underside of a hedge, black beneath its topping of snow. Neither colour nor movement. No early spring out there. Someone was singing. She got up and walked stealthily towards the sound. In the kitchen, Sophia was moulding cakes on a baking tray, singing 'Tomorrow shall be my dancing day'. She looked over her shoulder at Anita and said, 'No long faces. Go out and come in again.'

Anita did as she was bid, but managed only a crooked smile. 'This is the best I can do.' She sat at the table and watched her aunt. Sophia was wearing the bright patchwork gown in which she had first greeted her Christmas guests. She had folded her hair back and secured it with a whorled ceramic clasp; the effect was to make her look more composed and formal. Anita remembered a phrase much favoured by her Great Aunt Edith: One must honour the occasion.

'I was doing this while I was waiting for your mother,' Sophia said.

'You'll have a long wait. She's only just gone into the bathroom.'

Now that Sophia's face was free of the straggling hair one could see that the skin was criss-crossed by tiny lines, not driven deep, but like scratches on old parchment. What interested Anita was the bone structure. In the broad planes of this face she saw how her mother must have looked when the skull was not so fully fleshed.

'We don't want instant coffee at a time like this, do we?' Sophia took a bottle of wine from the dresser. 'All my consequences have come home at the same time,' she said as she handed a glass to Anita. 'Your mother has business with me.' She made a wry face, like a child who has undertaken something quite outside its capacity and hopes the adult world will understand.

Anita said, 'A ticket to Tahiti? You'd have time while she is assembling herself.'

Sophia sat opposite to Anita. There was a bowl of hyacinths on the table and the scent tickled Anita's nostrils. She sneezed. 'I'm not ready for spring.'

Sophia waited.

Anita said, 'Last night I was a child again. I can't explain.'

'Never mind explanations, tell me. And then you must get out of that wretched dressing gown and put on something more suitable.'

It was the unlikeness to her mother of which Anita was now aware. This was a person one could not pigeon-hole, classify, contain by a few terse comments. Anita's defence against her mother's vehemence and loquacity was the crisp, concise rejoinder. That wasn't going to work with Sophia.

'What was this child doing?' Sophia asked.

So I am to be the one to talk, Anita thought, to give myself away, to lay myself open to the terse comment. Can I bear that? She reflected on this, reminding herself that she was trained to deal with just this sort of situation. What was required was a psychologist's report, unemotional, objective and, above all, distanced.

'She was going round an art exhibition with her father. He knew a lot about art, but it wasn't the sophisticated, critical, assessing kind of knowing that most people respect nowadays. He appreciated and applauded; every stroke of genius dazzled him. He looked at each Picasso as though the paint were still wet on it. He dodged about, viewing from every angle, trying to catch the painting unawares and exclaiming with delight. He was a big man; he bumped into people and got into their line of sight. Some were annoyed, others amused. He interrupted conversations. One woman was telling her companion how much she adored Chagall and he said, "Yes, yes, he has a great sense of fun, but it's a pity he has to fill every space." '

She stopped, short of breath, aware of the sensation that spaces in herself were filling up. Her hands, those most betraying of members, were knotted tight together.

Sophia said, 'And the child?'

'She didn't realise how much she could learn from him, not just about art, but the way of looking at life.' In spite of the clenched hands something was happening internally over which she had insufficient control; she began to speak more quickly, sensing she had not much time. 'She went home feeling a bit out of sorts with him and herself, not quite knowing what was going on. Then, when they got home, they found that her mother had invited people from the tennis club in for drinks.' She fought back tears as desperately as if she were on a sinking ship, shutting doors, closing bulkheads. 'She was showing off and making silly jokes about balls and back-handers. The father moved among them as out of place as he had been among the people at the exhibition. But he listened.' She bit her lip and the eyes streamed; she mopped the eyes and the throat muscles strained, the nose watered. 'He listened far too intently while they talked about how old Jock always drove down the middle; he looked as if he were eating up their faces, which wasn't the studiously casual response they understood. It was the artist in him, of course, not noticing the mundane words but fascinated by the bones and teeth and eye sockets.' There was no way of preventing dissolution; the last control went and Anita abandoned herself to crying, the words barely distinguishable from the rending sobs. 'But she couldn't see it, she couldn't understand. She only knew that her parents were an embarrassment to her—the mother because she showed off and the father because he showed up. She hated them both.'

Sophia watched dispassionately until the storm ran out; then she said, 'Why was it so dreadful, do you think, this one incident which must be typical of things that happen to so many children?'

Anita said bleakly, looking at the hyacinths, 'All that promise never realised.'

'Promise can be renewed.'

Anita shook her head. 'I began to grow away from my parents after that. It didn't matter about my mother. Our relationship depended on arguments, back-answers, protest and counter-protest—

that intensified. What I had with my father ended there.' She shouted as if Sophia might interrupt, 'Don't talk to me about renewed promise. It wasn't just a stage that I passed through. Do you understand that? I ended there. The world shrivelled and wizened. And when, much later, I made a break the best I could do was to shack up with Terence.'

There was a long silence while Sophia looked down at the grain of the table, not reflectively, but as a place to rest her eyes.

Anita said, 'Well, no words of comfort from you. Thank you for listening—if that's what you were doing. But I don't suppose you took much of it in. You've no idea what it's like to live in a space that is getting smaller and smaller. It's terrifying. I'm well beyond comforting myself with bowls of hyacinths.'

Sophia sipped wine. For a time it seemed she would not answer. Anita looked at her with loathing, thinking, I've sicked up my guts for you and all you can do is enjoy a glass of wine. And she did seem to be enjoying it, savouring each sip, meditating upon its quality.

At last, Sophia put the glass down, but seemed reluctant to turn her attention from it. She ran a finger lightly round the rim of the glass. Then, 'Your experience has certainly been different from mine,' she said.

'Your mother and I were born to parents who didn't show off or stand out. They were rather dull. Our mother would have liked two nicely behaved, quiet little girls—small adults would have been her preference, I think. Until we were ten we were taught by a governess. I'm afraid all that we learnt from her was that education was one enormous yawn. A time of day was set aside for supervised play and in the evening our mother read to us from suitable books. We didn't have other children to play because we had each other. Except for the time we spent in this cottage with our grandmother, we were very bored and under-occupied. I couldn't believe everything was as muted and well regulated as in our home. I ran away in order to find out—just for a day here and there. I spent long summer hours with a gypsy family. I don't suppose they were very clean or honest or any of the things the Romany lovers romanticise about. What I loved about them was that the children weren't set apart; no one played special games with them or talked a special language in front of them. They were members of the tribe. The most frightening thing in my life was when I was made to realise (after my parents discovered where I spent my time) that I couldn't be a member of the tribe. It took me some time to accept that the gypsy way wasn't the way for me; but I learnt from

200

them and that knowledge was stored away deep, inside me.'

Anita said with some urgency, 'How long? How long before you found what was your way?'

'I would have been in my thirties.'

'Why so long?'

'I suppose I wasn't ready. How can one tell? The last thing we understand—if we ever do—is our own inner process.'

Now Anita sipped her wine and considered.

'And Mother—did she come with you when you ran away?'

'No. She thought one had to go much further than the gypsy camp on the heath. She saved up her money in a china pig so that she could get to faraway places.'

Anita said, 'That's sad.'

Sophia got up. 'But today we are not sad. So you must go upstairs and change your clothes.'

Anita went and soon returned in a neat black dress enriched by a rainbow scarf which did much for the dress but made little impact on the raw, swollen face.

Florence entered a few minutes later, ominously immaculate in kilt and white blouse. 'I shall have my breakfast first and then we will talk,' she said.

'There's porridge on the stove,' Sophia replied. While Florence breakfasted, she took the cakes from the oven and arranged them on a wire tray. Their spicy smell mingled with the smell of the hyacinths.

'Gingerbread?' Anita asked.

'For Andrew, who thinks I'm a witch. Try one, Florence, they're delicious hot.'

'It would stick in my throat.'

Tobias, who had appeared from nowhere, had no such inhibitions.

'He's unnatural, that cat,' Florence said. She added her used crockery to the pile on the draining board.

Sophia said, 'We'll wash up once a day to conserve hot water.'

'In that case,' Florence opened her handbag and took out the carving of the boy with the dancing bear, 'It's time we talked about this.'

'Then we should go to the shed,' Sophia answered calmly. 'Will you fetch Nicholas, Anita? He's in your father's room.'

*   *   *

Early that morning, Thomas had walked over to a neighbour's house to telephone Sophia. Now, very correct in these matters, he had written letters of condolence to Florence and Sophia.

'But we shall see them,' Frances objected, tense as a rebellious schoolgirl, black-browed and hands fisted. 'Surely, we shall go to see

202

them.'

'Later, perhaps.'

'I'll deliver them,' she said, jauntily assured.

He looked at her, rubbing a finger against the side of his nose, bewildered by the changing expressions of her face. His own features had long since ceased to keep pace with feeling.

'There isn't any other way for them to get there,' she appealed, eager now.

'Or for you to get there?'

'I'll just drop them in their post-box.' Now pleading. 'I promise. And I'll take Andrew and Jasper with me.'

He looked consideringly down at the letters, marvelling at the instability of youth, impossible to hold as quicksilver. She thought he was more like a soldier than ever, contemplating whether to send a patrol out on a dangerous mission.

'It isn't the letters we are concerned with, is it?' he said without looking up.

'I suppose not.'

He sighed and handed them over. 'As long as you are careful my dear. No, no!' He held up a hand, seeing her face darkening. 'Not that. But don't give everything to someone who will always reject.' It troubled him to think that this should be her early experience of love, fearing it would weaken the zest for living.

'Why do you say that of Nicholas?'

'Because he's the sort of man who is no good to a woman.'

She said steadily, 'I can only promise not to be careful.'

He looked at her in surprise and suddenly smiled. It was a moment of understanding which they had never shared before and no words were needed.

He watched them set out, all three delighted at their release.

Andrew said, 'Where are we going?'

'To the gingerbread house to deliver letters.'

'That's not very far, is it? I 'spect Jasper'd like a long walk.'

'After we've been to the gingerbread house, we'll go to the Hoopers' and make sure everything's all right there.'

They walked beneath great oaks still bearing their wounds in scarred trunks and lopped limbs, a few upturned like huge mops. Andrew and Jasper ran ahead, playing hide-and-seek.

As she walked, Frances was thinking of Konrad and Sophia. It was during the hurricane that they had got to know Konrad; previously, he and Sophia had been careful not to socialise. 'Why doesn't he come to see you when he's there?' Frances used to ask Thomas and Margery, curious about Sophia's companion.

'A matter of honour,' Thomas had said.

The hurricane blew away honour. For days they were without water as well as electricity and Konrad came down to fetch water from the stream. Then he and Thomas got on to the roof to pull tarpaulin across the great gashes. Sophia's cottage had suffered comparatively little damage and it was there that she and Margery cooked meals for them all. Frances remembered Konrad at that time as a big, brawny man who enjoyed the physical labour. He told her that his grandmother had been a high-wire performer in a circus.

'You're having me on.'

'No, no.' He was quite shocked. 'I remember a picture of her, on a rope ladder, in spangles, with thighs like tree trunks.'

'Didn't you ever see her—apart from the picture?'

'I may have done; but before I was old enough to store anything here.' He tapped his head.

Margery had been calm and Thomas effective during the hurricane and it was thanks to them that Frances and Andrew had not been unduly frightened. But it was Konrad and Sophia who enabled them to enjoy the aftermath. Margery was too unaffected a person to pretend to be other than dismayed and Thomas was anxious about her. Konrad and Sophia behaved as if the whirling demon which had struck down giants and ripped off roofs were a part of the natural order—or perhaps it was that they believed in disorder? the older Frances wondered. Whatever the answer, they had been tremendously reassuring. There was a lot of laughter in that cottage.

Frances knew that Thomas and Margery were deeply attached to each other, but, shadowed by the death of Jonathan, they were feeling their way, day by day. The spontaneity of response which so often reveals the nature of a relationship was lacking. It was Konrad and Sophia who first made her aware of a kind of loving that was different from the breathless discomfort she had experienced when she was with Jonathan. There was robustness in their exchanges as they worked together, an awareness in the way they looked and listened, combined, most puzzlingly, with a certain taking for granted which at times expressed itself in abruptness and even indifference. That Konrad delighted in Sophia's vagaries was shown in the way he watched her as she stood in the open doorway gazing at a robin on a branch, a tray of steaming baked potatoes held in her unheeding hands. To him, this vision of Sophia seemed well worth one half-cold potato. Frances, working with him and Thomas to clear a path through a tangle of torn branches, had been annoyed. But he liked his food and at other times when his expectations were disappointed he could huff about like a great tormented bear. Or a dereliction of duty might infuriate him so much he would mimic her in a way Frances thought horribly childish. He loved to hear her praised. When Frances admired one of the necklaces she had made, he said, 'You like it? You think it is very fine?' eager, as if her approbation alone could set the seal of approval on it. Sophia, for her part, would sit by the fire in the evening, hands clasping her knees, her pleasure in listening to Konrad talk revealed in the deep satisfaction with which she watched him. But there were times when, unaccountably, she would tire of this and walk out of the room leaving him in mid-sentence. 'You have no idea,' he had said to Thomas on one such occasion, 'what a challenge it is to love a woman who has absolutely no interest in you at all.'

As she walked through the shadowed snow, Frances remembered seeing them on autumn evenings, frost riming the fallen leaves. They had walked holding hands, not talking. That deep silence had been what most impressed her and what she would always remember about them.

'I don't know what it is you had,' she said aloud, as though they still walked there, 'but I want it—and I will have it.' She vowed she would not be like a Victorian heroine letting vitality die within her; she would make sure she stayed alive however long it was that she had to wait.

But as they drew nearer to the cottage, she was overwhelmed by the longing to see Nicholas so that all her wise intentions deserted her. Her heart beat faster, her nerves shrilled; she was cross with Andrew and shouted at Jasper. Her lips parted at one minute as if to laugh, the next they snarled as the dog thrust against her. When the cottage came into view, she made Andrew stand by the fence, holding Jasper in case Tobias should appear, and she was glad when Jasper barked because surely Nicholas would hear and understand and come rushing out. She noticed that for the first time this week the curtains were drawn back in the shed and she glimpsed Florence and Anita. They might all be there, but no one came out. Her face bleached, and had anyone been with her they must have thought her about to faint. She put the letters in the box outside the cottage door and walked slowly up the path, feeling they were all watching her, perhaps staying out of sight so that she could not intrude where she was not wanted. Her cheeks burned with humiliation and she clenched her hands as she turned her face to the wintry scene.

Paintings lined the walls of the shed; their colours were strong, the figures boldly executed, so that, although at first glance they seemed to catalogue disaster, the main impression was one of tremendous energy.

'Why, it's the Challoners' house.' Florence stared at a man on a gaping roof, a mug of tea in his hands, seemingly unaware of the devastation that surrounded him. Other paintings depicted people similarly unobservant of their surroundings—a grimy street, discoloured washing on the line, contrasted with the brilliant, excited face of a boy on a skateboard; a man trimmed his roses in the last of the evening sunlight as the sky darkened with parachuting figures; a woman baked in a house surrounded by soot-blackened warehouses; a girl laid her doll in its cot while the roofs of distant houses were tipped with flames. Florence put her hands to her face and turned away, but on all sides the figures blazed from their frames. 'It's too terrible,' she cried, staring at men crouching in the corner of a hideous factory yard, intent on their game of dominoes.

'But think of the courage it took to get it down.' Anita was excited. 'To order, compose...'

'And something else besides courage?'

Sophia suggested.

'You!' Florence rounded on Sophia. 'You and Konrad.' Suddenly, she shouted, tearing away the bonds of control, her face mottled purple. 'Anita, Nicholas, look at her standing there so cool and unashamed. You should want to kill her for doing this to me.'

Nicholas said in a cold, uninflected voice, 'He came here to paint. You didn't want him at home.'

'It was the paintings I didn't want, the bloody awful paintings.'

Sophia said, 'He was his paintings.' Although she spoke calmly, the tenseness of her body revealed her apprehension. She had put her treasures on show.

'Dear God,' Florence said. 'What has happened to me?'

Standing there, in the centre of the room, it was as if she had come on stage to find herself in an unfamiliar play. She was, above all else, a performer, and to find that she had got the performance wrong was deeply disquieting. She felt as if she was about to be found out, revealed as not belonging, inadequate at some very basic level; and there was something worse, some fear that she had never been able to identify. She saw them all looking at her, Sophia, Anita, Nicholas; not one of them moved to help her. She was alone. How had it come about when her entire life had been spent ensuring that this moment could never happen?

'You came down here because you "needed space",' she said to Sophia. 'What need had you of Konrad, you who had to be solitary? He was my husband. It was important to me that he was there. He belonged in my life.'

'He was there for you, Florence, for what you needed.'

'A person can't belong in two places at once.' As the assertion settled, something occurred to her and she cried out, 'It was because I told Father that you went to the gypsy camp. You meant to repay me for taking away your precious freedom, so you took Konrad.'

Sophia swayed as from a blow. 'No, no.' A hand went to her heart.

Florence watched her sister, now bent and shaken. She said, 'It was revenge.'

'No, it was never that, never!' Sophia's voice was hoarse and she seemed to have difficulty in breathing. 'That was cruel of you.'

'Cruel. Did you expect me to be kind and consider your feelings? Is that what you think is due to you?'

Sophia straightened slowly, as a person will who is recovering from cramp, afraid that any unconsidered movement may bring on another spasm. 'No.' She moistened her lips. 'Nothing is due to me and you have a right to be cruel. But please don't talk of revenge. I was grateful to you for telling Father.'

'That wasn't the way you behaved at the time.'

'Not at first, but later I was grateful. You helped me to see that running away with gypsies was a childish fancy.'

'You hated me.'

'No, Florence, never.'

'Why else would you have done it?'

Sophia ran her hands slowly down her face. She seemed perplexed by the question. 'I didn't think of you, Florence. It was wrong of me, I see that now. But at the time, I hardly gave you a thought.'

Florence stared around her, unable to comprehend what was being said. 'She never gave me a thought,' she addressed Anita, but Anita had turned to the paintings.

'We met at an exhibition. It was years since I had seen you. Konrad told me he needed somewhere to paint. That was how it started.'

'And are you telling me you had no idea how it would end?'

Sophia smiled. 'Oh, I knew how it would end, I don't deny that.' The smile was not triumphant, but tender, a tenderness which was private and excluded Florence. To Florence, it was as if her sister had said: this is something about which you can know nothing. She lashed out.

'You lied and deceived me, you and Konrad. It was sordid, squalid. Do you understand? Squalid.'

'Konrad never lied to you, Florence.' Sophia was angry and made no attempt to hide her contempt. 'He was always very open. If you had ever made enquiries about his painting holidays, he would have answered honestly. But you never put the question.'

'I was fed up with his paintings. I wasn't going to gratify him by asking questions.'

'They are accepting something!' Anita's voice vibrated at a pitch Florence had not heard in a long time. 'These people are all accepting something.' She was going from painting to painting, her face agitated by the unhealthy excitement that fairy stories had aroused in her as a child and that had led Florence to impose a ban on them. As soon as she had been round the room once, she started again, her eyes devouring each painting as if she could not have enough of it.

'Madness,' Florence said. 'I always sensed it. There must have been madness in his family.'

'But they are so wonderful,' Anita exclaimed. 'Can't you see, don't you understand? Mother? Nicholas?'

Florence thought she looked unhinged,

face flushed and eyes feverish. 'Look, look! He isn't emphasising the weird, the menacing. That man on the roof isn't trying to pick up the pieces after chaos; he's savouring the first gulp of tea, the warmth going right down to the pit of his stomach.' She darted from painting to painting, fingers stabbing, as if a demon had been released in her. 'The boy on the skateboard, the child with her doll. See them! They are so intensely alive. It is here and now. It is always now in these paintings.' Her voice cracked.

Florence said, 'I think you had better go and lie down.'

Anita ran over to Nicholas who was at the far end of the room. 'Surely you can see. What we call ordinary and humdrum was precious to Konrad. It springs out of all these paintings.'

Nicholas said drily, 'Something else springs out of these two.' He was looking at two portraits of Sophia, painted when she was some twenty years younger, the intense gaiety of the face invested with the artist's love of her.

'No,' Anita said. 'Not something else. The same thing—acceptance, now.'

They stood looking at the portraits for a long time in silence.

At the other end of the room, Sophia and Florence stood facing each other, oddly alike, hair tumbling out of comb and clasp, eyes insistent, mouths eagerly open. Sophia said, 'I never hated you, Florence. I understood why you told our father about the gypsy camp.'

'You left me on my own, and you knew Mother wouldn't let us have friends in to play.'

'Yes, I know.'

'When I played with the kitten, Mother said it gave her a headache. She made me practise hem-stitching.'

'Poor dear.'

'Then, when they realised you had run off, they shut me up in our bedroom while they talked. Mother said I mustn't think of myself all the time. But there wasn't anything else to think about.'

'Was that why you tore up all my books?'

'I had to do something.'

They were talking quietly now. They might have been replaying the past, trying to make a better version.

'You could have set fire to the room,' Sophia said. 'That would have made them attend to you. Remember how they reacted when we tried to have a bonfire on Guy Fawkes night.'

'There were the two of us, then. I couldn't have done it on my own. I have always needed company. I'm a sociable person and I have always made a place for myself in society.' Her voice became childishly cross. Sophia took her hand. Florence said, 'I had always taken it for granted that there would be people; that's not unreasonable, is it? I had not envisaged the supply running out.'

Anita said to Nicholas, 'Can't you see? The pain and terror aren't the last word. Konrad worked from chaos to order, from despair to hope.'

He found nothing but pain as he stared at the paintings, thinking of his father and wishing he had made better use of their time together. He turned away to the window and stood looking out on the snowy scene. Anita saw the expression on the strained face change to one of sad perplexity. As she moved beside him she caught a glimpse of Frances walking slowly away from the house to where Andrew waited for her at the garden gate. She said teasingly, 'When you are old and grey and full of care, you will want a hearth to warm yourself beside.'

He said, 'There are other things. When I was sitting with Father, I came across a copy of John Buchan's *Sickheart River* on the bookshelf. It reminded me that I've never explored that part of Canada. It would be interesting.' She saw that his mind was beginning to circle the familiar foothills of all his travelling—finance, equipment, timetabling.

'He gave them to you?' Florence's voice

rang out. 'Nicholas, Anita, she is saying that Konrad gave these paintings to her.'

'You didn't want them,' Anita pointed out.

'I should still like to have one good reason why you should have them, Sophia.'

'I like them.'

'That doesn't seem to me an adequate reason.'

'To me, it seems the only reason.'

'But you're no longer young, Sophia. What happens to them when you pass on? I hope you'll have the grace to leave them to Anita and Nicholas.'

Nicholas said with unexpected firmness, 'They are Sophia's to dispose of, if that is what Father wanted.'

Sophia laid a hand on her sister's arm. 'Florence, I would like to found a gallery where they could be exhibited. There would be other paintings for sale, of course, but Konrad's would be on permanent display.'

'Galleries spring up overnight and disappear as quickly.'

'His paintings are going to be valued.'

'I doubt that very much. I tried to have one of them valued once—the man was not at all encouraging. And even supposing you're right, and had the money, you could never run a gallery, you haven't the expertise.'

'I think Frances could run one, judging by

217

the changes she has brought about since she went to work in the bookshop.'

'Frances?' Nicholas said.

'She's a very capable and determined person. She would soon acquire what expertise is required for anything she set her mind to.'

'And the money?' He seemed disconcerted. 'These ventures do cost money.'

'Thomas might be prepared to put up the money. He would like to do something for Frances.'

'I seem to be excluded from these considerations.' Florence was becoming distressed.

'You didn't want Konrad's paintings in your home,' Anita said. 'You can hardly object to their being on show in a gallery.'

'And I should play no part in it,' Sophia assured her sister. 'I should hand over all the paintings.'

Florence looked at her in disbelief. 'But you like them. How could you let them go?'

'Because, as you have pointed out, I have no right to consider them mine.' She made a little gesture with her hands, as if offering a gift to her sister. 'Any more than I have a right to consider Konrad mine.'

'Not one painting?' Anita asked. 'You won't keep one painting for yourself?'

Sophia turned on her angrily. 'If I kept one

I might as well keep them all.'

'That is unnatural.' Florence's voice was at its most declamatory. 'We have to hold on to what we love.' She incorporated Nicholas and Anita in one proprietary glance.

Sophia said fiercely, 'Love is a matter of letting go.'

'Letting go, letting go, I am sick to death of all this letting go,' Florence burst out. 'Bad things come of letting go. You don't just stay still, you get carried somewhere you didn't want to go. Look what happened to Konrad. He let go and from then on it was as if his illness drew him like a magnet.'

Sophia seemed to recede from them. She did not move but one had the sense of a turning away; the signs of conflict and response in the body ceased, the hands became still, the shoulders dropped. 'It is too soon to talk of these things,' she said, quite lightly, as if putting aside a bill she had no intention of paying immediately. She looked at her watch. 'Poor Tobias will think he is never to be fed.'

'It would be no great matter were that cat to miss a meal,' Florence said, but Sophia was already walking away.

Florence stood between Nicholas and Anita and the door; the brother and sister reacted nervously, as if trapped. Florence said, 'This will bring about a change in our lives, you do realise that?'

Anita said, 'Yes, Mother, I do realise it.' She took Nicholas's hand. 'But now I think perhaps we should all go and have lunch.' They circled Florence to reach the door and she swivelled, her eyes considering them.

'As if she was wondering which one to pounce on,' Anita said, her voice a little hysterical. 'But we got away, Nicholas; we got away, didn't we?'

Florence, alone, stood transfixed, an expression of utter astonishment on her face. Wherever her eyes rested, impending disaster leapt out of the paintings. She scarcely looked at the central figures which had so impressed Anita. In her mind, another figure took their place. As a child she had had a recurrent nightmare in which a great tower that shadowed her dream house was about to fall. She had been too terrified to cry out, lest she precipitate disaster. Once, half-waking, it had occurred to her that even had she been able to summon help, neither her parents nor Sophia could have stopped the tower falling. That had been over fifty years ago; the tower had been a long time falling.

*   *   *

Frances and Andrew had been to the Hoopers' house and Frances had tested the central heating, proving, rather to Andrew's disappointment, that their electricity had not been cut off.

'We should have had to empty the freezer,' she said as they set out for home. 'And you wouldn't have found that very interesting.'

Jasper ran ahead, nosing in the undergrowth, and then backed away from his find. Andrew, who had followed close behind, halted suddenly and Frances coming to them saw an old dog fox lying rigid, the head thrust forward, making a last foray among dead leaves and rotted roots; snow tufted the whiskers around the bared teeth.

Andrew said, 'P'raps if we took him home and wrapped him in a blanket?'

'I don't think so, do you?'

He bent down and stroked the stiff bristles as though by touch he hoped that life might be restored. Jasper had run off in search of more lively game; in the distance, they heard him thrashing about and snorting as he did when pleased, then he was gone out of earshot.

Andrew hiccuped, the noise shockingly loud. He put a hand to his chest.

'You ate your breakfast too fast,' Frances said.

He hiccuped again, even more violently, and doubled up. Frances comforted, 'It'll be all right; just hold your breath and count to twenty.'

The spasms came too fast for him to

contain: his hunched body jerked from side to side and Frances, impelled by a need to share his pain, did what she had never before dared; she closed the distance between them and put her arms around him. He stiffened, but she held him until after a few more racking hiccups he buried his face against her shoulder. His breathing gradually became easier until they seemed to breathe as one.

They breathed and they alone. Frances was aware of how still it had become. Jasper must be far away by now; it was unusual for him to leave Andrew, in whom he took a jealous interest. If other creatures were abroad, they stirred no branches. Not one flake of snow fell. No bird sang. It would have been possible, had one been of a nervous disposition, to be a little afraid.

Light flickered. Frances, turning her head in the direction of that brief shadow play, saw a stag standing beneath an arch of branches. It seemed to her that he was the most natural creature she had ever seen, so completely did he belong in the space he filled; and she was struck by the courtesy with which he accepted their presence, his stance, despite the imperious head, so graceful and the eyes mild. She wanted to tell Andrew, but she knew that if there was any movement the stag would go. And, indeed, he was gone in a matter of seconds. No sound marked his passage.

Andrew looked up at her. 'You've stopped breathing.'

She said gently, 'I think we should be on our way now. Do you want to bury the fox?'

He nodded and she let him scoop the first handful of snow on to the arrowed head.

'We'll go back now, shall we? Grandpa will be wondering where we are.' She put an arm lightly round his shoulders and they set off.

They were surprised to find that the forest was full of activity. Busy little vans festooned with trailing branches, Land-Rovers bearing ladders and coils of wire, ploughed through the snow; men shouted to one another from high in the trees.

'It's all right for some,' one of them called down to Frances.

'If you get our electricity back we'll stand you lunch,' she answered cheerfully.

She and Andrew were walking close, jolting each other companionably, as they came to the garden gate where Jasper waited, muzzle comically masked by snow.

CHAPTER FIVE

No one spoke at breakfast except Florence. 'I have been making plans during the night. Someone has to look to the future. There

223

will be a lot to sort out in the house. You'll have to come back for a time, Anita. Terence will understand—selfish though he is he can't fail to see that it would be impossible for me to manage alone. Perhaps in time we might find somewhere for the three of us? It would be a wise move. Terence is not reliable and one day you'll find yourself alone and you know you've never been able to cope on your own. I haven't liked to say this before, but now is the time to speak plainly. And you, Nicholas, will have to deal with the business side.'

It's like being under machine-gun fire, Nicholas thought, pouring coffee. He was glad he had trained himself to pick out distant noises from the surrounding hubbub—outside the window a blackbird fluted and he heard every note.

Anita thought: she is like a vampire; it's not just comfort she wants, it's our life's blood.

'Solicitors make such a meal over even the simplest estate. You remember Mildred Percival and how ill she became when there was all that trouble over probate or whatever it is one has to wait for. I, of course, am not a depressive like Mildred. No one has ever seen me go weeping down the high street with my dress open to the belly button, or ever will. But I have borne a much heavier burden than Mildred, who had only to visit the hospital once a day for a matter of months. All the worry and upheaval of Konrad's illness has taken its toll—running up and downstairs until I very nearly had a heart attack and we had to move him down to the sitting-room; special meals to prepare; making sure that wretched doctor was doing all he could (and I'm still not sure that he did, but that can wait). You don't know what it was like, Anita; you only dropped in in the evenings on your way home from work. You should have taken compassionate leave; it was false kindness on my part not to insist. But I shall insist now, for your good as much as my own.' She took a fourth piece of toast and dug a spoon deep into the honey pot.

She doesn't know what she is saying, Sophia thought; this is her last stand against her fears.

'And it wasn't just Mildred Percival. Look what happened to Josie Symonds. If it hadn't been for her family—all so supportive, the Symonds young—I shudder to think what would have become of her. I don't like talking to you in this way, don't think I do; but you've been so sheltered, so shielded from unpleasantness, you've never had to take up your responsibilities and it's only fair that I am straight with you now, I would be failing as a mother if I weren't. I remember Josie Symonds's daughter saying to me, "I should never have forgiven myself if I had failed Mother at this time." Her husband, of course, was very supportive too. You must remember to point that out to Terence. It would be good for him to model himself on Harold...'

A mirror, Sophia thought, that's what we are, her mirror; without us she would cease to exist. She has no inner life. I never understood that it wasn't selfishness made her fight for attention, that it was her only way of survival. When she sits before her mirror each morning she sees no reflection. Ever since she was young, she has refused to look in the mirror until her hair is brushed out. Then she will raise her eyes and begin to create a person. She has never examined the raw material. My poor sister, we have all expected too much; it wasn't her fault that she had a big, forceful body and a timid soul.

★   ★   ★

Anita had gone for a walk, Florence to her bedroom. On the half-landing Florence had looked down on Nicholas who had just emerged from the kitchen carrying a wicker basket full of logs. 'I'm going to need a lot of help, remember.' She had then proceeded to her room, shouting for Sophia. Nicholas began to make up the fire, listening to his mother telling Sophia, 'This can't go on, this pretence that nothing has happened to change our lives. There has been a very big, a profound change. We have to discuss what arrangements need to be made.' He did not hear Sophia's reply; it was either brief or cut short by Florence. 'These last months have been a terrible strain on me, a torment. I was strong for Konrad's sake, but now I'm exhausted. I can't go on any longer. Do you understand me? Do they understand me, my children? It's I who must be cared for now.' At this point, a door had been closed.

Nicholas finished tending the hall fire, his face expressionless. He took a small hearth brush and began to dust the wood ash into a scuttle. Tobias, who had been observing him from the sitting-room doorway, came and played with the brush and for a time Nicholas amused himself with the cat, delight brightening his usually guarded face. He squatted on his haunches and parried blows with Tobias; then he rolled over on his back and held the cat in the air above him. Tobias, wild with excitement, lashed out with paws which, for once, were ineffective, so expertly was he held. 'It's not fair, is it?' Nicholas said. 'Come on, then. Show what you can do.' He let the cat down on his chest, whereupon Tobias decided that there was nothing he wanted more than to be a lovable cat and he lay with paws outstretched across Nicholas's shoulders, in an ecstasy of purring and dribbling. Nicholas stroked him and whispered in his ear. Eventually he sat up, cradling the cat in his arms. 'We'll go and make a nice fire for you in the sitting-room, shall we?' Tobias, who didn't much like change when he was comfortable, dug in his claws and spat. 'I know, I know,' Nicholas soothed as he carried him into the sitting-room. 'They never let you have peace, do they, these restless mortals. And you so small you can't wrest it for yourself.' He continued to soothe Tobias, amused and tender, while he built up the fire.

Nicholas was so occupied that his usually acute hearing failed him and he was startled when Anita spoke from the doorway.

'Nicholas, I'm going.'

She shut the door and leant against it. Turning and seeing her there, he thought she looked as she had years ago when they were children and she planned to emulate some great adventure she had read about in a book. His face twisted as if she had hurt him.

'Going where?' he asked, adopting that tone of indifference with which he had made it plain he was not going to play her game.

'Away, now.' She came forward eagerly, the absurd hair, the exposed face, making her intolerably childish. 'This evening. I've asked the men who are mending the telegraph wires to give me a lift into town.'

He wedged a log firmly in place. 'You can't go away before the funeral, silly.'

'I can and I must.' She stood over him, compelling attention.

He said wearily, 'Oh, Anita, go and play somewhere else.'

'Come with me, Nick.' She crouched beside him. 'I've found out where Konrad was born—a small town in East Germany.'

'We knew he came from Germany, didn't we?' The flames leapt up and he sat back on his haunches, dusting his hands on his thighs. Tobias, who had moved away in a huff, watched from the far side of the hearth.

'Sophia says he had a grandmother who was in a circus—a circus, imagine that!—and he remembered his mother saying she was Russian and came from Vlonsk.'

'Vlonsk?'

'Well, that's how it sounded. I've got it written down somewhere.'

'That will be a great help. A circus performer, from Vlonsk—somewhere at the turn of the century, perhaps? There must be a lot of people who will remember that.'

They were crouching on the hearthrug, knees touching, in what should have been companionable proximity; yet it was now that she saw how far away he was. Behind the lashes which formed a lacy curtain to the eyes, there was a glimpse of steel. Uneasy, she leant forward and gave his hand a little shake. 'I don't want to trace our family tree, stupid. And I certainly don't expect to walk down a street and have the sense that here is where I belong. But a part of us was formed by people who came from these places. Don't you want to see where Konrad and our great-grandmother were born? Surely you can understand; you make journeys which are of far less personal significance. It's our memory, Nicholas; the memory that we should have allowed Konrad to give us.'

'He didn't have much in the way of memory himself and what little he had, he can't give us now.'

'Now more than ever, perhaps.'

In the firelight, her face glowed with the innocent simplicity of a child. He said, 'We can talk about this after the funeral.'

'No, it has to be now.'

'What about Terence?'

'I'll leave him a note. His senses are very acute and I suspect he's already making his own arrangements.'

'And your job?'

'The Council will be only too happy to find that one of its educational psychologists has taken voluntary redundancy. You have none of these problems, you always travel light. Come with me.'

He pursed his mouth primly. 'We couldn't possibly leave Mother before the funeral. I'm surprised you can even think of it. It would show a lack of respect for Father.'

'Oh, Nicholas, how can I make you

understand! Imagine yourself given the chance—a once-only chance—to visit the place you most wanted to see, the most remote, the most secret, on the condition that you left immediately. You would recognise an offer you had to close on without havering or backward glances.'

'There is one flaw in that analogy. This place would have had to fire my imagination—not my sister's. As far as I'm concerned, no chance has presented itself here, no offer has been made. You've been working yourself up into a state ever since we arrived. Mother always said you were very highly strung as a child; she was forever having to make sure your mind wasn't overstimulated.'

'Are you agreeing with her that there might be madness in Konrad's family? Well, that's a risk I have to take. When I looked at those paintings I realised how joyless my life has become. A pensionable job and an available man—I so very nearly settled for that. Those paintings turned everything upside down.'

His lip curled, giving his usually sensitive face a spiteful look. 'One thing seems fairly constant in all this.'

She drew back, her eyes glancing from side to side as if seeking something she had overlooked. 'What do you mean?'

'When you left home you said you weren't

ready to be on your own—hence Terence. Now you're leaving Terence you're looking for another prop. You do understand what I mean?'

'This is different,' she said sharply. 'It's natural to want to share it with you. We came here, the two of us; I felt we should find our way out together.'

He raised his eyebrows, mocking her. One of the logs crackled and she plucked a spark from the rug. 'Havering, is it?' he said. 'Having a few backward glances, are we?' He got up and went to the window. 'The undertaker is coming tomorrow—did you know? There's quite a lot of cloud now.' He opened the window and leant out. 'Smells different. A thaw on the way.'

She got up slowly as if her limbs had stiffened. Her face was that of an adult confronted by defeat.

'I'm sorry, Annie,' he said. 'Truly, I am sorry; but we're a bit old now, you and I, for escapades.'

* * *

Florence met Thomas in the wood that afternoon. She was on her way to his house to thank him for his letter. 'This sort of thing should be done personally,' she had insisted at lunch.

'He didn't express his condolences

personally,' Anita had pointed out.

'That was delicacy.'

He was still being delicate this afternoon and seemed disposed to discuss the puzzle of the pony *ad infinitum*. Apparently he was returning from a round of visits aimed at finding its owner. 'One or two people were out and I dropped a note through their letterboxes, so it's possible that one of them...'

'I would have thought you knew every pony in the forest.'

'I concern myself mainly with legal matters affecting the Commoners. And I don't socialise much. Neither does your sister. I didn't recognise half the people at the party and I certainly wouldn't know their animals.'

Florence was convinced that this was no chance meeting and was determined that they should not let a golden opportunity pass them by. She marvelled at the generosity of life. Here, at the time when she most needed it, was this man, a widower, saddled with an unappealing grandson and a sullen, self-appointed housekeeper. And as if that were not cause enough for rejoicing, he was personable: tall and upright, not lacking energy, and with a promise of humour—a good, salty humour at that—in the slant of eyes and lips. How little faith she had had. There are circumstances to which some are suited, others not. She was not suited to living alone and her needs had been realised. There had been no call for panic. Long before Konrad died, before he was taken ill, even, a new life was being prepared for her. She had scarcely understood her decision to come to the forest when Konrad was dying; now she saw that she had been guided here. This was one of those things which had to be. She could see herself years hence talking of her late-found happiness to a friend—'God has kept this good wine until now', or some such apt quotation. There could be no other reason for Thomas's presence in the vicinity of her sister's cottage, let alone on this unfrequented path at this particular moment. She felt an hysterical desire to cry out and shout loud hosannas.

'You must let me take your arm,' she said. 'The snow has turned to ice on the soles of my boots.'

They made slow progress, for Florence had a lot to say before they reached his house, by which time she hoped to have disposed of Frances and the boy, a boarding school in his case, she thought.

'Of course, you understand all that I'm going through.' The words had been so long waiting she could not hold them back any longer. 'It's a great shock to find oneself alone. To be alone is not a natural state for a normal, healthy person.'

'I'm sure your family ...' She could have

234

wished him to take her point more immediately, but at least he sounded gently concerned.

'Oh, the young will flee. It is natural for them to spread their wings.' She remembered, too late, that his son had chosen not to spread his wings. How tiresomely the events of his life conspired against her efforts.

Thomas, who took her to be referring to Frances, said brusquely, 'We wouldn't want to hinder them, would we?' thereby hoping to discourage any attempt on her part to give advice.

'Oh yes, indeed, we should never rely on the young.' Florence regarded this as the opening she needed and went on with feverish haste, 'I have friends—as I am sure you have—who sit around counting the days to their children's next visit. All their arrangements are provisional. "Of course you will understand that if Debbie or Jamie come down that weekend we shan't be able to manage it ..." "Yes, we would be delighted provided we don't have to go to Debbie or Jamie to mind the children, paint the house, feed the animals ..." Quite pathetic. And such a mistake to cling to the company of the young. One must find companionship among kindred spirits of one's own age. I have no time for the elderly who talk about being lonely. They are the sort who wait for people to come to them. I have always been impulsive, I have to reach out to others.' Instinctively, she tightened her grip on Thomas's arm.

Thomas swung his stick in a circle, a habit Florence found irritating in a man. 'I'm sure you have a lot of friends in Chiswick. One mistake which people in our situation make is to move away from the area where they have established themselves. Wouldn't you agree?'

Florence lost no time in disposing of this. 'One must be enterprising.'

'Exactly my point.' Thomas took her up enthusiastically. 'So, even more important to stay where there are likely to be the most opportunities for enterprise.'

'But one must accept change.' Florence made a gesture towards the transformed wood with her free hand.

'Life provides the changes,' Thomas mused. 'We, on the other hand, must ensure the stability—old friends, local interests...'

God, but the man was obtuse. Florence could barely control her impatience. 'The main interest of Chiswick was the District Railway line which enabled Konrad to get to work easily.'

'Your dramatic society,' Thomas continued smoothly. 'The tennis club.'

'Fewer and fewer parts as one gets older.' Florence was beginning to feel the cold creeping from legs to thighs, sending probes into her stomach; she had not eaten well at lunch. 'And club life, while nice as a bonus, is scarcely a foundation for an interesting old age.'

'Quite.' Thomas paused to poke his stick into a tangle of branches which seemed to have offended him.

Florence sensed her moment. 'A woman needs someone to care for.' She had some experience of putting this sort of line across and never had she done it better, the little tremor which was beyond her control adding much to the poignancy.

They walked on in silence for some time while Thomas meditated and Florence anticipated. Eventually: 'Hospices? Had you thought of that? Visiting and so forth?'

She removed her hand from his arm. When he ventured to look Thomas saw that she was crying, her face crumpled and ugly. He was dismayed, but the instinct of self-preservation was strong in him. 'A bad time this for you,' he said, taking her elbow, but addressing his remarks to the path ahead, instinct telling him that eye contact was to be avoided at all costs. 'But you will find your way. One does. Not much alternative. It's that or go under, and you're not the sort to go under.'

It was gloomy now and no light glinted in the sepia hollows between the trees, while above them the snow lay thick as felt on the arched branches.

After a time, Florence said in a dull, conversational tone, 'My son announced this morning that he is going to the north of Canada. The bleaker the landscape, the more it appeals to him.'

Don't weaken, Thomas urged himself. Not far to go now; a few hundred yards and the house will be in sight. He swung his stick again. 'You will come in and have a drink with us?'

Florence thought not. Frances would be there and would see that she had been crying. 'I merely wanted to thank you for your expression of sympathy,' she said formally. She declined his offer to walk with her.

He watched her go regretfully, knowing she needed help and that he had rejected her. If only she had not been quite so outrageous ... He was aware of a surprising and inexplicable gratitude.

Florence was thinking: Not the sort to go under—he made me sound like an inflatable woman. As she turned to a wider track a woman appeared suddenly out of the gloom. She had fair, curly hair which had probably served her well all her life without her having to make much effort and the sort of face which has grown pleasant by habit. 'Another merry Christmas behind us,' she said with wry good humour.

One of those women who make the best of things, Florence thought, swept by a gust of resentful anger; the sort who are grateful to eat the crumbs from the rich man's table. As she went on, having barely acknowledged the friendly greeting, she felt faint with rage. There was no sun. The air no longer had any bite but seemed more bleakly cold. Here in the wood, everything was grey. This was the dismal aftermath of shining days—days of invigoration and intense activity; skaters, their bright scarves flying like flags; the rush of air tearing one's hair and filling one's lungs as the sleigh careers downhill; the walks with leaping dogs and stumbling, happy children ... All gone, the sparkle and the gaiety; the tumult stilled, brightness obliterated.

*   *   *

It took the combined efforts of Nicholas, Anita and Sophia to prevent complete collapse when Florence returned to the cottage. 'You should have had a proper lunch,' Anita shouted angrily as her mother stumbled about the hall, wheezing and crying at the same time. It was difficult to get her coat and boots off because she kept clinging to her helpers and grabbing at them whenever they seemed about to move out of arm's reach. Eventually, they managed to get her into an armchair with her feet propped on a stool, a blanket wrapped around her. Even then she complained of the cold, and brandy and a hot-water bottle did little to revive her.

Nicholas built up the sitting-room fire. Sophia said to him, 'We shall need more coal. I'll get it.'

He looked up, about to say that he would do this, then noticed how drawn her face was. He followed her into the hall.

'You probably need a respite from all of us. If going out to the shed is your form of retreat, go ahead. I'll see to the coal later.'

She had her hand to her side and seemed to be breathing with difficulty, her face putty colour.

'What is it?' he asked, concerned now.

'It's only that I'm used to living alone most of the time. I get into a silly state when I have people on top of me. Something inside me begins to feel as if it's trying to claw its way out.'

He put an arm round her bent shoulders. 'These last days must have been very hard for you and we haven't been considerate guests.'

Florence called from the sitting-room. 'Where is everyone? Why have you all left me?'

Sophia straightened up. 'Dear Nicholas,

240

bless you for understanding. I'll go out to my retreat now.'

In the kitchen, Anita was preparing food. 'A lightly boiled egg and a plate of bread and butter and she'll be all right,' she said to herself, not knowing whether she believed this or even cared.

'Where's Sophia?' she asked Nicholas when her mother had been persuaded to eat.

'She went out to get more coal.'

'Shouldn't you be doing that?'

'I think she wanted a chance to get out.'

'And she's not the only one.' Anita went out of the room and could be heard going slowly up the stairs—scarcely the tread of someone about to make a break for freedom, Nicholas thought with wry satisfaction.

He sat opposite his mother, nursing Tobias, who had had a troubled day. His instinctive sympathy was with the cat. In his view animals behaved impeccably in comparison with humans.

*　　*　　*

Sophia stood at the door of the wood shed, looking up the garden. The snow was now scaled like a fish except where it lay smooth in the violet shade of the hedge. A magpie perched guardian of the gate, the only creature. Beyond the gate the trees had regained their skeletal structure, the winter

241

blossom gone from many of the branches, though here and there tufted whiteness brushed against the pale clover of the sky. It was freezing again and the soft breath of snow falling from branch and roof had ceased. It was still, as if time had stopped; but she felt moisture in the air on her face and knew that this scene would change soon. Tomorrow the fish scales would fill with water and gradually the land would emerge. In time, the forest would green, but not for her. She looked at the scene as if familiarising herself with every detail, studying its composition, remarking how the snow imposed a simplicity on the landscape, learning the changed contours of her world.

She stood there a long time while the shadows crept towards her, deeps of blue from which a tree stump rose like the funnel of a sunken steamer. On the other side of the hedge, and between the bars of the gate, the sharpness of outline blurred into a mist of pink and grey shot through here and there with a sheen of palest turquoise.

As she looked at the gate, the old excitement stirred in her, fiercer than ever, and she marvelled how gates concentrate the mind. She was aware of past and future gathered here, of the company of other women who had, and would, stand at this door, looking to this gate.

Although it was only a little after three, the light was failing. Anita had now missed the men who would have given her a lift into the town. As she watched the dwindling of the day, her lack of belief in herself was more acute than ever. How selfish I am being, she thought, picking at flaking paintwork with a fingernail, wretched and yet somewhat comforted by her wretchedness because it provided a justification for inactivity. How could a good daughter, or even an indifferent daughter, ever think of leaving her mother at such a time? She got up listlessly and rummaged in a drawer. Presently, she went to the bathroom where she washed her hair. This was something she always did when cornered by circumstances which seemed beyond her control, whether professional, personal or merely domestic.

As she came out of the bathroom, Nicholas called from the hall. 'Phone call for you, Anita.' She wound a towel round her head and went down the stairs.

Terence's voice came over the wire, the choked-with-emotion voice he had used when she found out about Thelma Armitage. 'I was in such pain when you came I scarcely knew what was happening; I had a terrible time after you flounced off. Then I waited all day yesterday expecting you would come

243

again, or at least phone. But I understand now. Nicholas has just told me that your father died.' There was silence; when she did not fill it, he went on, 'Darling, I'm so sorry. I really appreciated him, you know. You can't believe how miserable it is to be lying here, not able to do a thing ...' He was trying hard, but as he was tone deaf to his own feelings, the more effort he made the more insincere he sounded. 'You are there?' he asked anxiously.

'More or less.'

'I've been wondering—I realise this may not be the moment...'

'If it's the car that's worrying you, I haven't done anything about it.'

He made a noise between a moan and a whinny. 'I was wondering whether we oughtn't to get married.'

'Married?'

'Well, it's been good in patches over the last few years, wouldn't you say? We've outstayed most of the couples we know. We understand each other pretty well. I'd say we're suited.'

'Why now, Terence?'

'Lying on one's back, helpless, makes one more aware, I suppose. When you went flouncing off—which you certainly did—I thought: this will happen once too often if we don't do something about it.'

She was becoming conscious of how softly

244

he was speaking. 'I can't hear you very well, Terence.'

He said agitatedly, 'I can't shout, for Christ's sake!'

She had a mental picture of him, head cocked, listening for noises on the landing; if he shouted Mrs. Carteret might hear and Terence liked to keep all his options open. She said, 'I quite understand. I can't say too much at the moment, either.'

He said petulantly, like a little boy who is sick and half afraid, 'I need you, Anita.'

'I'll be in touch, Terence.'

She went back to her room and began to brush her hair. This is my grandmother's house, she thought; the house to which my mother came as a child. Perhaps Sophia will leave it to me and it will become my house. Looking in the mirror, she saw that the room had become her frame. The mirror was old; her grandmother must have looked in it, probably her mother, too. How could one hope to break out of this frame? Certainly Terence had not been, nor ever would be, the answer.

'You will break my heart.' The voice startled her, for it was her mother's; but she had spoken the words at another time than this and had certainly not intended them to relate to her daughter's present situation. How long ago had Florence said this, and why? Undoubtedly, it was in childhood, for the phrase, which becomes banal with usage, had carried all the implied terror of real breakage.

The mother had a tendency to dislike her daughter's friends. 'That's a rather common little girl—I hope you're not going to learn from her', followed by the mimicry at which Florence was so expert. Or: 'Darling, she's so intense. I really don't like these intense friendships. They are not healthy.' After which she would constantly interrupt their play, swishing into the room with vases of flowers or in search of an imaginary book (she was not much of a reader). 'How solemn you two are! No laughter. Don't young girls laugh any more?' 'Secrets?' she would shout when Anita protested about this interference. 'Oh, I don't like *that*. What have you to be secret about?' These exchanges gave rise to a longing for boarding school which Anita's reading led her to believe was a place where secret pleasures might be enjoyed endlessly. Her mother's reaction to this suggestion had done nothing to dispel the illusion—in fact, Florence's rejection hinted at secrets of a darker kind than any Anita could conceive. Once, when they were by the seaside, she had made her way into a famous girls' boarding school and hidden in the locker room, just as if she expected the great building to set sail with her in it. It had been after she was handed over to the police by an unsympathetic games mistress that her mother had said, 'You will break my heart.'

It seemed to Anita as she looked into the mirror, that those words which, had the child only realised it, had been spoken heedlessly at the time, nevertheless contained in them the answer to a mystery. All her childhood she had seemed to stand on the wrong side of a door which was guarded by a magic phrase and would open only to someone bold enough to disregard its warning. Florence had shown the way through when she said, 'You will break my heart.'

Anita got up and, edging backwards as if something terrible would happen if she turned away, moved out of the mirror's frame. She stood in the corner of the room, waiting, her own heart seeming ready to break.

Somewhere below a door opened; there was the sound of footsteps ascending. Nicholas called from half-way up the stairs, 'Anita, Mother wants to know why you're hiding away up here.'

Anita came as far as the landing and looked down at her brother. 'I've been washing my hair.'

'Could you put the kettle on. Mother would like a pot of tea.' There was a fleeting expression of triumph in his eyes, an awareness that she had submitted to his judgement. Anita said, 'Yes, sire.'

When he had gone, she went to her father's room and looked down at the still form. She had no sense of his presence and had not expected it, but she knew that he had loved her, so she said, 'You came alone, not knowing why or where; pray that I have a little of your courage in me, something of your sheer cheerfulness of spirit.' She saw that her mother had replaced the carving of the boy with the dancing bear on the shelf. She picked it up and took it with her.

In her room, she towelled her hair dry; then she packed her case with a quick efficiency which would have surprised her mother. On the landing, she could hear Nicholas and her mother talking in the sitting-room so clearly that it was apparent that the door must be open. Impossible to get down the stairs carrying a suitcase and hope to give a reasonable explanation if detected. But as this was an enterprise wholly lacking in common sense, it seemed appropriate to take the risk that it would fail at the very beginning.

She was half-way down the stairs when Tobias, who was sitting in the hall, caught sight of her and began to yowl loudly. Anita hurried back to the landing, heart thumping, mouth dry, overwhelmed by a sense of retribution awaiting her, of being caught in an ultimately unforgivable act. The sitting-room door opened wider, then Florence's voice said sharply, 'Do you respond so immediately to humans every time they mewl or cry?'

'Humans can get their own supper.'

'But it may not be supper they are crying out for.'

The door slammed to, an expression of Nicholas's irritation which effectively cut him off from Anita. 'A good try,' she whispered as she passed Tobias. 'But it didn't work this time.' He made a noise in his throat, difficult to tell whether a curse or God speed.

It was not fully dark when Anita let herself out of the back door. The sitting-room curtains might not be drawn, in which case her mother or Nicholas would be able to see her as she went up the garden path. She must make for the shelter of the trees at the back of the cottage. This would mean starting her journey on an unfamiliar track—or, worse still, having to make her own track. She set off aware of the fact that she had no idea where she was going or what would become of her, and with few other facts at her disposal.

As she walked she became aware of something else, a change which had come about. Although the walk was as uncomfortable as she had anticipated—she stumbled over twisted brambles, dislodged snow from branches so that it trickled down her neck, her case got heavier and heavier—a tension had snapped and she felt pressure eased around her skull. A light breeze whispered and was answered by a sigh among the trees as if some discomfort were subsiding. It was possible to imagine that not only the workmen but the forest itself was going about the business of restoring normality and it seemed a part of this natural process to see a woman leading a pony coming towards her and to be greeted with friendly cheerfulness, 'Are you lost? Can I help?'

'I have to get back to London,' Anita gasped.

'Then you're in luck.' The woman looked at Anita with such genuine pleasure she might have been seeking someone whom she could benefit. 'My sons are going back to London. They work in the City and believe that their merchant bank will founder if they're not at their desks tomorrow morning.'

'This pony is a miracle worker,' Anita said as they settled the case on the broad back. 'Every time he appears something wonderful happens.'

'Well now, it's not the way I've thought of Tufty until today, because he's naughty and obstinate and will wander. But this time his wanderings took him to Thomas Challoner.'

She did not say why this should be in any way wonderful, but she stroked the pony's neck fondly.

Anita said, 'I'm surprised Thomas didn't know it was your pony.'

'You know him? But, of course, you must be the person who found Tufty on Christmas Eve. Definitely we owe you a journey. As for Thomas, we haven't had much contact. He has always seemed so remote until today.'

'How old is Tufty?'

'Seventeen. My youngest was four when we first had him. It will be lovely to have a child ride him again.'

'Andrew?'

'Yes. We've agreed that Andrew should ride him whenever he likes.'

They walked in silence for a time and then the woman asked, 'Where in London?'

'Holland Park. But your sons can drop me anywhere once we get within hailing distance of London.'

'Nonsense. You shall be taken to your very door.'

There were three handsome cars in the clearing close to the house and inside it, in varying degrees of impatience, waited her three tall, dark sons.

They insisted that Anita should have tea, over which it transpired, unsurprisingly, that her hostess was long-widowed.

'You must give my good wishes to

Thomas,' Anita said when she set off. 'I didn't have time to make proper farewells.'

'Shall I telephone Sophia and let her know that you have a lift to London?'

'Please—but later, say in an hour.'

The woman made no comment. Anita could tell that she accepted all that had happened this day as a gift, not to be questioned.

Things will not be the same again, Anita thought, as she sat in the car of the third son. She was a little frightened by the way in which her journeying had been taken out of her hands once she had made up her mind to it. But she did not look back on the forest as they came out into open country.

* * *

'They'll be back soon,' Florence was saying when the telephone bell rang. Nicholas had been sent out to find Anita, who, Florence said, could not have gone far—'She is not in the least intrepid and will already be regretting this piece of nonsense.' In spite of this assertion, she stood very still, holding her breath while Sophia went to the telephone. From the words overheard it was not possible to gain a clear picture of what had happened.

'Well?' she said, when Sophia returned.

'That was Mary Kingsland—the owner of

the pony.'

'Blast the bloody pony!'

'It seems Thomas dropped a note in her door. She thinks it may have been you she met on her way to claim the beast.'

'I passed a woman, certainly, but that is neither here nor there.'

'On her return, some time later, she met Anita.'

'And?' The gravity of her sister's face was not reassuring to Florence. 'Why didn't Anita have the grace to telephone herself?'

'Because she is on the way to London with one of Mary's sons.'

Florence sat down. For a long time she was silent, then she said, 'There's something odd about the timing, wouldn't you say?' She might have been trying to fit together the pieces of a puzzle. 'It must have been before three o'clock that this Mary Kingsland and I passed each other. It is now nearly half-past six.'

'She said that Anita set out some time ago. The pony had to be settled and she couldn't phone earlier.'

'Even so, they must have spent quite a long time together, Thomas and this Mary.' She had the palm of her hand spread out before her, examining it carefully as though reading the life line. Sophia pressed the tips of her fingers into the hollows of her cheekbones. For some moments they sat quietly, each contemplating the mysterious interweaving of beginnings and endings in the woof and warp of their lives. Then Florence made a fist of her hand. 'Our numbers do seem to be dwindling, don't they?'

'Nicholas should be back soon.'

'But not for long.' Florence looked around the room, studying it critically for shortcomings which were not hard to find: frayed upholstery and cracks in plasterwork, improvised lampshades and other indications of impoverishment. Sophia thought of Nicholas, who would go away still bearing the burden of an unexamined childhood.

Florence said, 'I have always needed company. That I acknowledge. It is part of the human condition, isn't it? And if I have been more dependent than some, it is surely a very human failing. It's not a sin to be gregarious.' She spoke as if ticking off from a list things that must be said. 'And if I have a dominant personality, is that my fault? I dare say I haven't given all the thought I might have done to other people's requirements. But which of us does? My husband didn't provide me with what I needed—nor I him, it would seem. That is by no means unusual in a marriage. As for my children—well, children are by nature ungrateful and no doubt I made mistakes, making mistakes is the lot of a parent.'

There was a long pause. Sophia pressed a clenched fist against her mouth, her eyes enormous in a face growing more shadowy in the dim light. Florence said, 'I suppose you would say that I have never made my own life. How can I now?'

'How can you not?'

Florence looked at her sister speculatively, as she might inspect an item at a sale. 'Are you happy here? It was all right when we were children, but it's so cramped and not at all comfortable.'

Sophia, withdrawn into her corner, looked as if she would have liked more space between herself and her sister.

Florence sat up straight, her chest thrust out. 'You know you can't go on living here when you get older. I notice you're already looking rather frail. You'd better come back with me. I have always been the stronger. I shall be able to look after us both. We are older and more sensible now. I dare say we could live together quite happily. I'm sure that is what Mother would have thought appropriate.'

Sophia looked at her, eyebrows raised, and Florence returned the look defiantly. The corners of Sophia's mouth began to twitch, her nose wrinkled like Tobias's. Some internal insurrection appeared to be taking place in Florence; her eyes started out from their sockets, her cheeks bunched and her face grew red. Sophia doubled up, forehead on knees, shoulders shaking. Florence said, 'How can you?' But it was no use, mirth overwhelmed the small display of anger. It was some time before either was capable of speech, but at last Florence gasped, 'I haven't laughed so much in years.' Since their mother was no longer here to ask, there was no need to rack their brains as to why they were laughing.

Sophia's face had become very pale. It no longer seemed so well firmed, as though in some intermediate stage, not yet changed by illness but become a stranger to vitality. Whatever Florence's next demand, it seemed unlikely she could summon the resolution to resist.

Florence said, 'Nicholas won't always be able to go running off to faraway places and Anita will certainly discover she can't manage on her own. I shall have to keep the house going for them ...' In spite of her exhaustion, Sophia's senses were still sharp. Now she detected something mechanical in her sister's delivery, as though she were going through the motions of a game. Where had she heard this note before? It was the flickering light on the wall that gave the answer. The treasure hunts their grandmother had organised for them—the house in darkness save for firelight casting gnomish shapes on walls and ceilings. Florence had worked hard at the treasure hunts, though with a strange reluctance to come to the right place, as though she feared that what she might find would not be treasure in her terms. As she came towards the end of all her explorations, she would say, 'Might as well try here—it's not very likely, but we ought to look,' finding yet another excuse for delay before making the final discovery.

The lamp was burning low, but neither of the sisters wanted to move. The firelight flickered and Florence, too, watched it; it gave her pain and reminded her of fears which she had not understood and never would now that they had been consigned to memory's keeping. In the last few days she had carried out a very thorough investigation; every door had been tried, every lock tested, each window and corridor examined. She felt a kind of satisfaction at having researched so exhaustively, a pride in a project well executed; nothing had been overlooked, every alternative had been pushed to the limit. Now, drained of feeling, hands resting limp in her lap, she was aware only of a great emptiness. She said, 'So, how am I to manage on my own?'

Sophia, about to dredge up an answer, checked, recognising a difference. This question was not addressed to her; Florence was asking it of herself. She got up quietly and went to the window. The night was still, no moon or stars, only the faint glimmer of the snow; too dark to see the gate. She drew the curtains.

'I'll make tea,' she said.